WHAT KEEPS US APART? (PART 3)

Susann Svoboda

PROLOGUE

When you fall,

or you are pushed over,

know that you *can* get up again

as long as you believe ...

No, not in unicorns.

Believe in *yourself* :)

~ 107 ~

Melissa looked blindly at the documents in her hand. They felt like a thick, heavy book. She did not see the writing, did not read the contents. But she knew they meant an end. The end of her marriage to Lyle.

Would she still recognise his voice from afar? Could she still catch his aftershave from across the room? Or was all that already lost in the past? Her breath was weak, her stomach once again tightened painfully at the thought of him. Just like every time, every day, even months later. She had done everything this time to distract herself from her broken heart. Had given her everything to put her ideas into action. Lyle, oh there was his name again in her thoughts, yes Lyle had paid her a generous salary, she herself had held several jobs for months and because of that she had managed to do a lot more in that time than perhaps normally would have been possible. Most of the time she hardly had time to think of herself, let alone anything... any*one* else. And yet she always felt this emptiness as soon as she was at home. As soon as she was *alone*. With whom could she celebrate her success? With whom could she talk about her greatest joy? What she had achieved in the last six months was an absolute dream for her and for the children she wanted to reach. She combined her passion with the need to help other children and perhaps also to show them how art gives you the opportunity to live out your own imagination and represent it in a way that you choose. In *her* new company they can create, make, experiment with all kinds of colours, papers and materials and let their own stories, ideas or fantasies run wild. She offered them different classes to draw, paint, craft or just try new things. Melissa rented one of the floors at a business block and gradually sought out employees who were good at working with children, whatever their ability, whatever their age. They could tell their own stories and Melissa would illustrate them. If they were still interested, they could also have them printed. Or the other way around, she would draw and they would tell a story. Either way, she hoped to give many children the opportunity to find themselves or just be a child. Just as she had found herself - art was a part of her life.

She could hardly wait to open her door to them. Then, once she started working, she wouldn't have time to think about him, would she? What did she miss, after all? His coldness, his mood? Him being near her. His arms. She often wondered if she should have stayed. Would they have been happy then, together? Would he have returned her love then? *Love...* you stupid, stupid cow. There had never been any talk of that.

There was a loud knock on her flat door. Mel flinched as if she had been caught daydreaming in class. She stared at the door. It couldn't be ...

Before she could even get to the door, it swung open and her new acquaintance, perhaps even friend, stepped in. Her red curls bounced on her head; her cheeks flushed from her morning jog. She looked full of life, as always. Content with herself and the world and she always did her best to make Melissa feel that way too. Tried to at least.

She was now standing in the small concrete flat that Mel had been renting again for a few months. With all her money now going into her business, there wasn't much money in surplus and this accommodation would have to do. It did. She had lived in old fashioned East German flats all her life. She didn't long for anything better at all. In fact, this one-room flat suited her well. It had everything she needed. A large living room as soon as you entered with an attached kitchen just to the right. And next to it a small bathroom with a shower and her bedroom. Either way, she spent very little time here, and when she did, she made herself comfortable on her little sofa and planned her next edition of magazines, which she still reliably put together and successfully delivered each month to children in all walks of life. Just because she no longer lived with Lyle didn't mean she would abandon the children's organisations. It also offered her even more distraction on those long, lonely evenings. No, where she lived was more than enough. What did she want a garden for, or a private beach, or an incredibly handsome man near her? *Mel!*

"Well, have you finally signed them?" spoke Patty as she had walked past her and unreserved, she grabbed a glass from the kitchen cupboard and filled it up for herself. Of course, she had immediately recognised what Mel was holding in her hands. She had spent many long nights just listening to Mel and cheering her up. She knew everything, well maybe not exactly everything. She knew 90% about her marriage to Lyle, just not the reason why she had married him in the first place. She was too ashamed to reveal it to her new acquaintance. What's more, it would be against the rules. Did that *still* matter? Damn right it did - it was the whole reason for this dilemma. He will *never* love *you*. That had been the deal. She got angry with herself again that *she* had actually fallen in love. Such a stupid thing to do.

Melissa felt the weight of those few pages in her hand again.

"I want to read them through first." she defended herself weakly. She felt that knot in her stomach again, that emptiness and that fear.

"Mel, it's been half a year. A whole *six* months!" said Patty insistently, stopping in front of her. They were the same size. And yet she suddenly felt small and unremarkable next to this colourful woman. Even in her sports clothes, she made sure to wear neon colours and all of that just emphasised her joy in life. Melissa wore only a pair of jeans and a boring T-shirt. They couldn't have looked more different. At least she had done up her hair a bit, into an amazing ponytail, that *was* something.

Patty shook her head and took a long look at her friend's face. The brown eyes still bore the pain and defeat of what this cold, ruthless man had done to his wife.

"I'm afraid it's not a trashy novel. You have your opening event the week after next, with the mayor! Clear your head and put an end to this. Use your chance of a complete fresh start."

She put her hand briefly on Melissa's shoulder, squeezed emphatically, and then she went back upstairs to her own flat on the third-floor.

Melissa knew she was right. Melissa had heard every word and agreed wholeheartedly. It was all just wasted energy and time; it wasn't a romance novel. Otherwise, he would never have let her go, would he? He would have come to win her back. He would have pulled her into his arms and kissed her passionately. Deep inside, a voice began to defend his side again. He had only just finished writing his book, so he had to promote it in all sorts of different places as best he could and make his presence felt. He had to do this book tour in America, it said so in his contract. And Lyle stuck to the rules, *all* of them. She was sure, he had signed a thousand books for the last few months, guaranteed, and read out loud individual chapters of his story to packed rooms in various bookshops. He hadn't had time to get her up at all, or think about her. And certainly would not have missed her. If she had stayed there, she would have seen him just as little. He spent weeks away from the house anyway, just so he didn't have to see her. He would never have wanted her back.

Melissa took a deep breath. Would have, should have, could have. She stood alone in her living room.

So no one saw her put the papers back in her drawer, unread and unsigned.

~ 108 ~

Melissa laughed on the inside, even on the outside, as her posters and name banners were placed on the windows and doors. She was so excited and so proud of her business. The design was a book and brush, just like the pendant on her gold chain, the gift from Lyle where he had first asked her to marry him.

And again, she had slipped into the past. Again, she pushed all those nagging feelings away from her and focused on the now. Don't let it get you down again, fight it, live ... *without* him.

Mel let go of the necklace she had involuntarily grabbed at her thoughts and straightened her shoulders. She congratulated herself even now on how well the picture and the name fitted. Melissa's Easy Art - Easy Heart was the beginning of an infinitely promising adventure.

She thanked the workmen warmly and went up to her floor. How that sounded - her floor! All the rooms and large hall here on the fourth floor were meant for her and her children. She had more than enough space, one room for each class. There were also smaller offices for her staff, so they were comfortable too. The last of the furniture and materials would be delivered over the next few days. In a week's time on Saturday, the whole town would gather here and see what she had done with the place. In doing so, she hoped to create a lot of interest and invite many new families.

When she got upstairs, her newly installed phone rang. She could hardly believe it. A call! Maybe a booking for next week? Maybe for the coming weeks?

Melissa couldn't hide her joy in her voice.

" Melissa's Easy Art - Easy Heart." she announced cheerfully. She smiled to herself. She stood alone in a still empty office. Only the telephone was already there, and the cables for the computer, printer and copying machine, etc. Everything else was yet to come.

"You want to file for a divorce?"

Mel was hit like a slap in the face. His voice. Her first feeling was joy and excitement. Hope. Then his cold tone filtered through to her.

She closed her eyes for a second.

"Lyle." she spoke breathlessly. That was all she could say at that moment. She didn't need to add anything because he immediately continued talking.

"How is it that I'm hearing about this from my *lawyer*? Don't you remember our arrangement? Who else have you told?"

"Of course, I remember our contract. Very clearly." she finally responded. His foul mood made her forget her own little joy and she matched his annoyance. "It's been a few months that I haven't heard from you. So why not a divorce then? We don't live together anymore anyway."

Mel could literally feel him struggling to keep his composure. He took a deep breath and exhaled loudly.

"That was your decision."

"Which I would make again." she countered immediately, even though her heart bled at the thought of their last moments together.

"Because of this Roger? I've given you enough time to amuse yourself with him, haven't I? That's enough."

Melissa had totally forgotten about that side of the argument. He had had nothing whatsoever to do with her decision. It had all slipped into oblivion. Only now did she remember his wounded pride. His sudden appearance on the beach where she had been standing with Roger. His accident and the hospital room. They were not pleasant memories. Everything had gone so wrong. And yet she couldn't accept his insinuations. He was still driving her *crazy*.

"Oh, you gave us time?" she mimicked him. "How generous of

you. Was that in the contract too? Willingness to let me have affairs? Is that why you didn't contact me either, so you could keep spending *your* nights with other women?"

Her anger suddenly took on new heights. This man, her husband, was incorrigible.

"Or just with Verona?"

There was a quaint silence on the other end. She could have screamed. Why don't you finally admit what happened or is still happening with you and Verona? Now I can handle the truth too!

"There will be no divorce." came the unequivocal answer and he hung up.

Melissa's heart was pounding in her throat. She was angry and sad and totally beside herself. If there was one thing she hated, it was when he upset her so much that she met his anger with the same fury. Why couldn't she control herself, and calmly discuss it like two adults? Surely, they could have sorted out all these misunderstandings right now, and either gone through with the divorce or given it another go. But no, they broke out into a rage out of nowhere. And neither knew more of the truth now than the other. And worst of all, she still didn't know whether he was having an affair with Verona or not.

~ 109 ~

Melissa had almost forgotten about the phone call. She hadn't run home and struggled with reproaches all evening. No, just a *little*. It had only taken her a day or two to get his voice out of her head again and concentrate fully on her work. She hadn't picked up the divorce papers a hundred times to sign them either, and put them back immediately each time. Just a couple of times, maybe. She hadn't lain awake all night remembering their good times together, as rare as they had been.

Oh yes, she *had*. The nights were the hardest. Still, and now only much more so. When she closed her eyes, his voice echoed in her thoughts, in her mind. Not always cold, not always angry. Mostly loving and so different from how he actually was towards her. Over time, her real memories mingled with her hopes. Especially when she was alone, and had no way of distracting herself. Then she dreamed of a second chance. Maybe he could love her after all.

No, that was rule number one. *No* love.

Why the hell did you have to break that particular rule? A little love affair with another man would have been so much easier to manage ...

Melissa stood nervously in front of her wardrobe. Today was an important day. She hadn't slept a wink and today she had to show hundreds of people that her new business was worth its weight in gold. Today she was going to prove to all these people that Easy Art Easy Heart could give hope and fun, for everyone. The mayor had signed up, along with journalists and other bookshops who might want to publish a collection of the children's drawings and stories. She was also expecting her former boss and colleagues, old acquaintances and, of course, lots of families - future customers, if all went well.

And she was going to dress appropriately for that. The problem was that, as usual, she spent all her money on others and didn't treat herself to anything. She had left all her elegant evening dresses at Lyle's house - for good and still existing reasons. She had no interest in re-entering his world and yet today would probably have been a good excuse to put one of those dresses back on. Clothes don't make the person, but one did feel a lot better in them, for the right occasion. She now chose the only suitable one in her wardrobe and set about making the most of her normal, plain appearance. A blouse and skirt had always suited her best.

Melissa stood among the people and felt at ease. Perhaps for the first time in her life, the crowds were not too much for her, she loved the hustle and bustle, loved hearing everyone talking - about *her* idea. She was pleased and smiled happily. She made the rounds and made sure that everyone had something to drink and eat from the light buffet she had ordered. But most of her time was spent with the families and the children, letting them try out different arts in the new rooms, helping them find good colours or draw something they were thinking about. She used pencils or paint however the children wanted and nimbly and skilfully drew their ideas, then she gave them the sheet of paper and they took turns. Their faces were open and happy. Mel's heart warmed. It was working out - just as she had imagined. Easy Art Easy Hearts all around. Finally.

For a moment she stood with the journalists and the publishers to emphasise the positive aspects there too. A few of the women were momentarily distracted from their cause. Their attention no longer seemed to be on the children, or on Mel, but on something else entirely.

Melissa followed their conversation as she was set to approach them and her step wavered.

"Have you heard about Lyle McClory? About his *solo* book tour in America?" asked the boss of the children's series, for which

Lyle had also written a children's book or two.

Shit. Why would they be discussing him of all topics?

"Did *you* know, I heard his marriage is falling apart any minute. His wife hasn't been anywhere near him for the last few months. Definitely not by his side."

"Maybe an affair?"

"Now there's a man I would never, ever kick off the side of *my* bed." came the excited voice, of the dark-haired journalist on the right. The other women only nodded in agreement.

"I'm dying to have a chat with him..." said the other and they chuckled softly.

Melissa fought with her heart, with her stomach. No affair, and yet a marriage in trouble. And no, she wouldn't kick him off the edge of the bed either. Everything inside her tightened at the thought. But it had been *she* who had left him.

She walked as confidently as she could towards these attractive women so that they would end their current conversation. She ignored the sinking feeling in her stomach and surprised herself. Her business was the most important thing, she couldn't think about anything else. The other women remembered their real task here and now gave Mel their interest again after all. Mel tried to concentrate on the interview, even smiled. But her body was trembling.

"Sorry I'm late."

Before she could do anything, or think of what her reaction should have been, she suddenly felt someone grab her elbow and pull her towards them.

In a lightning second, she recognised Lyle, who must have been in sight a few minutes earlier and that's why they were discussing *him*! Then her mind was lost. In that very moment he was kissing her in front of all those people. In front of the women who were suddenly speechless. Also a little confused. And infinitely *envious*.

It had only been supposed to be a subtle greeting, just a little hello for show. But that had utterly gone wrong. Her body was immediately torn back and forth with a thousand feelings, but above all she felt that hot fire ignite instantly. In that moment, that proximity wasn't enough and Lyle's hands urgently framed her face as to ensure the kiss continued where they were. It hadn't been necessary, for Mel didn't resist in the slightest. Her shock had been great, but the desire inside of her suddenly much greater.

He had seen her from afar, in her beloved blouse and a skirt, with her hair held tightly together, and he was lost. Her neck was so free, so seductively naked.

It went through them both like a shock wave. Neither of them would ever have admitted it, but at that moment there was only them. Mel didn't know how this kiss would have ended if the journalist hadn't interrupted them excitedly.

"Mr McClory, how nice to meet you here too. Do you perhaps have time for a short interview for our local newspaper?" Mel heard the voice behind her, knew this woman just wanted the first bit of gossip. She could bet the interview would touch on his marriage too.

Lyle looked into her eyes for another brief moment, speechless as to how she had triggered such a reaction in him. His heart was still beating hard against his chest. He wanted nothing more than to be alone with her *now*. With his *wife*. It suddenly seemed inconceivable to him that he had been able to be without her for six months. He had to have her. And soon.

"Maybe later, thanks." Oh man, his voice.

He grabbed a glass from the buffet table and drank it in one go. Melissa realised he'd been as overwhelmed by that kiss as she was. Too bad they couldn't talk about it now, lest *do* anything else.

His appearance and greeting had attracted more attention than she would have thought. They were suddenly the centre of attention at the party. Her mind was blocked, she didn't know what to say, how to face him.

Melissa stepped away a little and took a glass too, water would have to do. She needed a clear head, even more so now.

She didn't get to say anything. Out of the corner of her eye, she also saw the most important guest of the day moving eagerly towards the couple. The mayor of the town, who had made it possible for her dream to come true in this central location. With him by her side, she could more easily advertise and perhaps make herself known in other districts.

Gustav Walsh gave her a friendly nod, a glass of champagne in his hand, his cheeks already a little rosy from drinking during daylight hours.

"Melissa, you haven't introduced us yet," Gustav said invitingly. His eyes were shining, he had been watching the spectacle closely. He was not blind. The other women bustled around near them, curious to hear the answer.

"Lyle McClory. Melissa's *husband*." He shook the other man's outstretched hand vigorously and just then, the mayor realised who he was standing in front of. And that they were married.

Melissa could imagine what the others were thinking right now. *She*???? She was used to other women struggling to even comprehend why a man like Lyle would have married a woman like *her*.

Gustav laughed; his joy genuine. Melissa smiled a little uneasy. She needed to get a grip on herself as soon as possible and not internalise every single word her husband was saying and stop thinking about her lips, which she so desperately wanted to touch to simply relive that kiss. She didn't dare look in his direction. The fact that he was standing right next to her was excruciating enough.

"I can't believe it! But Melissa, how have you been able to keep such a secret? This is fantastic news for your business. I can see it in the papers now, the McClory Arts and Literature Foundation, that -"

Melissa was back on earth in one fell swoop. And immediately back to her full senses.

"No." she interrupted him rudely and quickly regained her composure. Her anger was not directed at the mayor, but at Lyle. She took a deep breath before continuing. "We keep our business arrangement separate.... Besides, the name is already on all the leases and advertisements. Melissa's Easy Art Easy Heart actually fits quite well, don't you think?"

Gustav looked at her a little quizzically, but didn't object.

"It can't hurt to mention your husband and his success here and there, though."

"Here and there, perhaps." she simply agreed. She struggled with herself not to stamp her foot and walk away.

The rest of the opening event went quickly and without further incident. But every time she turned around, she saw her husband with a journalist or a committee member and the anger inside her rose more and more. What was he telling them? Was he bragging about *his* fame? Had they all already forgotten what they were actually here for and did they all only see the writer Lyle McClory? Did he have any idea about her business here? What would people actually remember today, her or him? Oh, she wanted to be alone with him at last.

Finally, she had said goodbye to the last guest and the door fell loudly shut. The whole floor was in total chaos, but she didn't see that at the moment. She only saw him. He, in his smart, elegant suit, looked stunning as always. She watched him loosen his tie and take off his jacket, hanging it over the back of a chair. He ran a tired hand through his hair.

Damn it, why had he turned everything upside down? Instead of wanting to have a proper talk with him and being happy that he had finally come to see her, she was pissed off.

Melissa came up to him and stopped a few inches short of him. He looked at her expectantly. His look was friendly, he appeared to be smiling.

"Congratula-"

"What the hell are you doing here?" Her eyes sparked fire. She had watched everyone idolise him all day. Every person she spoke to after his appearance asked about *him*, even the children. She had had enough with pleasantries.

Lyle pulled his shoulders back, bracing himself for a fight. He certainly hadn't expected this reaction now that they were alone. Hadn't she felt the electricity, too, between them during that fleeting kiss? Had he been imagining it all? All day he had been unable to think of anything else. He couldn't quite follow why she was so upset.

"You see this? All of this?" She pointed to her floor, her rooms and posters. "I sacrificed *all* my time and money to get this up and running. *I* did this."

Lyle didn't doubt that at all, or at least not that part of her business.

"I can see that. And I just wanted to congratulate you on how far you've come."

"Yes, this far! And now you show up, the great Lyle McClory, and you drop *your* name everywhere."

"Mine and your name."

Melissa was not fazed. She hadn't used her married name on purpose.

"This is all for the children. I want them to want to come here and feel comfortable. As soon as they hear your name, expectations will fly higher and I don't want that. I want them to see how good they are without feeling the pressure of having to be as good as others. I want them to fit into *my* world, not yours."

Lyle looked at her crossly. He knew she had a problem when it came to showing herself with him. But the fact that she despised him for it made him angry.

"I am not the one who has too high expectations of herself. It's you who doesn't trust yourself to fit into this world."

She gritted her teeth, not wanting to hear his argument at all. It was much easier to stay angry than to give him a chance.

"What do you know about the world of ordinary people! You come here and turn everyone's head. All these months for nothing. Why did you come? Today of all days?"

There was sadness and disappointment in her voice now. The excitement of the day, the surprise of seeing him in front of her and the thousand feelings his appearance brought made her suddenly infinitely tired.

"Is it really so bad that children might aspire to be like *me*? I have written and published stories and novels all my life. And

I was successful at it because I never gave up. I've been writing since *I* was a child and some of those stories were good, some were bad. I would have loved to have a place like yours where I could maybe meet a real writer. And that's *not* beneficial to your children?"

Mel ran a stressed hand over her face. He had reminded her what she actually thought of him. How impressive his life really was, after all. She was suddenly ashamed of herself for not wanting to acknowledge his successes.

"That's not what I mean."

"I know what you mean. You wanted to cut me out of your life altogether. Your business, your name. And the divorce right on top of that."

Lyle grabbed his jacket. His gaze was cold but intense. He stood so close to her she could smell his aftershave. Her defences were weakening. Her body more and more restless.

"You're right." She admitted softly, but not what exactly he was right about. Her heart in her throat. Her hands damp. "It can also encourage children to believe in themselves, that they can be anything they want."

"*You* have achieved all this in a very short amount of time. What you have wished for. You yourself are also a celebrated artist, whether you acknowledge it or not. They will see you as their role model. They will want to be like you."

Mel was trembling all over. His words penetrated deep into her core. She believed what he said. He seemed so sincere. Did he really think that highly of her?

Lyle made to leave, but hesitated for a moment. His gaze still cold, yet somehow different. He grasped her left hand, ignoring the instant warmth that ran through him. He lifted her hand a little, twisting her wedding ring between his fingers.

"And the answer to why the hell I'm here..." he said quietly, looking up from her hand. Relieved that she still wore his ring. "You are my wife. *My wife.*"

And with that he let go of her and composed as ever, he walked away again.

Melissa stood rigid and frozen in place. She didn't know if she wanted to laugh or cry. Scream or sing.

She had imagined a thousand times what it would be like when he came to win her back. She had prepared all kinds of dialogues in her head and wanted to be able to say exactly the right thing for every moment. But she couldn't have imagined a day as screwed up as today. From a small yet hot kiss to an argument and accusations, to shame and regret and then ... hope? She was his wife, that's why he was here. Just his wife? Just because of the contract or was there more to it?

She should be concentrating on her business, should be enjoying the large number of visitors and interest for the first few weeks, but she was completely exhausted and couldn't form a clear thought. She didn't even know when or if she would see him again. Where did he live? What was he doing here? Would he *kiss* her again?

Melissa shook her head to stop her thoughts. First, she had to tidy everything up here again so that everything could start smoothly on Monday.

She had enough to do for the next few hours to distract herself. And then the whole mind game started all over again, into the night.

<h1 style="text-align:center">~ 110 ~</h1>

"So just a welcome kiss? On the cheek?"

Melissa was totally out of breath. What had she been thinking? Since when did she *ever* enjoy jogging? She was so unfit after all. Patty didn't look tired in the least, while Mel was eagerly looking forward to her little shower. It wasn't far now! Her cunning plan had backfired, instead of being distracted by the running and all the exercise, they were now talking incessantly about Lyle. Her ruffled up thoughts just went round in circles.

Patty wanted to hear everything in the finest detail, a second time.

"Mmmmh on ... the ... mouth..." admitted Mel. It sounded much worse as she couldn't actually talk, she was so knackered. She felt a stitch in her side but wouldn't let on or didn't dare stop, that was *never* an option. She looked totally weak and stupid in her friend's eyes again anyway. Let her at least think her fitness level had improved.

"That's interesting. Tongue?"

Melissa stared at her in shock. She almost tripped over the curb at her question.

"No. It was ... in front of everyone." But she knew only too well that all it would have taken was another millisecond and they would have *both* been in each other's arms. Just as in that moment, the fire had been kindled deep within her.

"Good." her friend said contentedly. She hadn't even broken a sweat. Mel could only imagine how she herself looked right now.

Thankfully, they had finally arrived at the front door to the block of flats and Melissa leaned forward groggily. She had persevered, even with the ongoing unpleasant interrogation. All she wanted to do was shower and fall half-dead into bed.

"Melissa." *Shit.*

She jerked back and stood upright. Patty's eyes sparkled as she stood right next to her. It was a strange reaction from her acquaintance and she wondered confusedly what she was up to.

Both women looked at him differently. Melissa would have liked to sink into the ground. She never, ever wanted to face him like that. She had to look terrible. After all these months, he should only see her in the best of lights. Not so red, sweaty, out of breath.

Patty's look was challenging, like a warrior she crossed her arms in front of her chest and lifted her chin. She seemed eager for a fight.

Lyle nodded at her and held out his hand.

"Hello, I'm -"

"Lyle, her soon-to-be ex-husband. I know." she interrupted him directly. Her eyes cool and dark.

Melissa swallowed nervously.

He dropped his hand. His gaze countered her dismissive gesture. Mel couldn't read from his eyes what he must have been thinking. She felt a bead of sweat roll down her nose. She rubbed her face, irritated. That hadn't helped.

"Excuse us for a moment." he spoke politely but firmly. Patty narrowed her eyes a little before giving them some space and making a beeline for the letterbox. She had no intention of going inside. She stopped within earshot.

Lyle turned away from her and pulled Mel with him a little. She looked gorgeous, even when she was as red as beetroot on her face. She had her hair jauntily in a ponytail and she was wearing skin-tight leggings and a top. He hadn't guessed how much he would be attracted to her. Had it always been like this? Oh yes, he had only chosen ways to always keep his distance at all cost; precisely because of this deep desire in him for *her*.

"You told her about the divorce too?" He tried to lower his voice, but anger brought it out colder and louder than intended.

"Not a word from you in six months." she repeated herself for the umpteenth time. "Yes, it seemed to make sense to get divorced. I hope you had a good time with your girlfriends."

"As you did with Roger!"

She shook her head aggressively. Again and again, he evaded the subject, simply not admitting to her what he had been up to. And with whom.

"I couldn't come sooner. I had my book tour - you know that."

"Really? It seems to me that it was really only the divorce papers that brought you here. If I hadn't gone to the lawyer, we would have put even more years into this pointless marriage."

"Melissa!" His tone warned her to tread carefully. He was very aware that other people could hear them, especially the overbearing friend. If looks could kill... "We need to talk this through properly. But not here. I'll be back tonight."

Melissa looked at him. She wanted to talk it over, yes, but maybe not alone, without witnesses. She wanted clarity, but maybe not. Was divorce the next step or not? She didn't know what was best for them anymore.

"Do you have a date?" Lyle had misunderstood her anxious look and searched her face for any give-aways of what she was feeling. A last bead of sweat burned in her eye. She rubbed her face in vain. Or was it tears?

"Okay."

"Okay? You have a date?" Lyle was all confused. She hadn't even heard his question; she had been so preoccupied with her mind turning on a thousand warning lights. She stared into his face. Her body however, ignored the lights. She felt this endless attraction between them. Did he feel it too?

"I mean, tonight is fine. Where? When?"

"I'll come here. I'm interested to see what you treat yourself to with our money." He nodded, looked up, evaluating the grey high concrete block of flats. He didn't look impressed, even a little arrogant at that moment. Feeling defiant, she stepped away from him. And with one comment, she felt she was no longer drawn to him. She moved away a little more in her mind as well.

"Anything else to add?" she asked challengingly.

Lyle shook his head silently. His expression was unreadable. He seemed to want to say something else, but didn't. Her heart was beating hard against her chest, and not just because of the exercise.

Everything else would just have to wait until tonight. *Everything* else.

He glanced once more at her friend, who had not taken her eyes off them. She nodded her head slowly, as if to say she was right. 'Future ex-husband'

We'll see about that. His eyes gave an equally confident response.

When the two were alone again, Patty put her hands on her shoulders.

"Wow, a perfect specimen of a man." she said laughing and then she stared at her friend extremely sternly. And with words she had never meant so seriously before, she brought Mel back to reality.

"Mel, whatever you do, don't sleep with him."

~ 111 ~

Her legs hurt. Her stomach was in knots. Her head was full of silly ideas and thoughts and fantasies and tasks and hopes. Aaaaarrrggghhh. Tomorrow was her first day at work. Tomorrow was the actual start of her business. And today she still had to talk to Lyle. It all seemed too much for her all of a sudden. Couldn't relax, couldn't sit, couldn't stand. She wished today and tomorrow were simply over already and she knew what her future might hold. If only she could look into a crystal ball where she could see if there would ever be hope for this love. If only she had the answer to that, then everything else would fall into place.

The doorbell rang abruptly. Like an omen of the mood that would prevail between them.

Melissa pressed the button to unlock the front door, then opened the door to her flat.

She was wearing black leggings and a T-shirt, having deliberately put on casual clothes so as not to give the wrong impression. In any case, she looked better than she had this morning. When she had finally taken a look at herself in her bathroom, she could have cried. Why was she the person who turned bright red as soon as she did anything sporty? It had not been a pretty sight. Here we go again.

He, however, looked as attractive as ever, in his jeans and T-shirt. It was so rare not to see him in a suit. In general, she was surprised to see him without being caught up in his work.

Lyle closed the door behind him and turned to face her. For a long, intense moment, they just stood in front of each other, not knowing what to do.

"Are we alone?"

Mel's shock must have been written all over her face so that he immediately shook his head, understanding that she had taken his question the wrong way. They had both probably been thinking of the same thing, because he knew where her mind had been racing to.

"Not for that." He laughed, what a sound. "Although -"

"No!" she replied immediately, seeking distance. What should have been a large living room suddenly seemed far too small, and the few pieces of furniture and belongings did *not* put enough distance and hurdles between them. She fled to the open kitchenette so that she had the counter in front of her and he was far away from her in front of the sofa.

He glanced around her domicile before his eyes sought hers again. He had to get to the point and discuss what was important before he lost his self-control. It was all right for her to be there with the glasses and the drinks having something to distract her. He regretted coming here instead of a restaurant where they would have automatically been distant and stay that way. What was to stop him....

Melissa clinked the glasses around clumsily, trying to spend as much time as possible with them before she finally had to give it up and face him again.

She carefully handed him the glass so that they didn't accidentally touch.

"I won't stay long. I know tomorrow is an important day for you."

They sat down on the couch and armchair, as far away from each other as they physically could.

Melissa smiled at his comment. The tingle in her stomach this time was at the thought of starting over tomorrow. She was so incredibly excited.

"I hope it all works out. I hope the children like all the activities. Have I thought of everything? Will my staff all come? So many things that can go wrong."

She bit her lip unnoticed. Something she often did without

knowing it when she was nervous. Lyle immediately looked at the glass in his hand. What on earth had possessed him to meet with her *alone*?

"Nothing's going to go wrong. I imagine you've made ten other plans, for every occasion or occurrence. It's going to be great."

Lyle knew her so well. Had she known that? Since when did he speak so kindly of her? This was the second time he had outright praised her. It was all driving her absolutely *crazy*.

Which was it going to be, divorce or not?

"You wanted to talk something over." she began timidly. She clutched the cold glass with both hands as if it offered her the only support.

"The divorce." he replied.

She felt a sharp stab in her chest. She had known exactly what was coming and also that it was the only solution, for both their well-being. And yet she had hoped that perhaps there was another way out than to cut him out of her life forever.

"Of course." Her voice sounded much stronger than she felt inside. She straightened up and went to the drawer. She had touched the papers so many times that she found them within seconds. "I have the papers here."

Turning back to him, she saw his uncomprehending look. She was confused. What exactly did he want and not want? She stopped next to the cupboard. The greater the distance, the better. That way he couldn't read the confusion in *her* eyes.

Her hands were shaking.

Lyle couldn't stay seated any longer and came towards her. Annoyed, he snatched the papers from her hand but paid no attention to them. His gaze was fixed solely on her.

"You're driving me crazy." he said coldly, waving the documents in the air. "Mel, the contract remains. We're married and we're going to stay married."

Mel wasn't quite sure what she was feeling. Anger? Fury? Relief? Hope? But why, he just wanted to keep the money and not her.

"You call this talking *properly*? It sounds like I don't have any say in the matter."

"That's funny coming from *you*! You just pulled the documents out of your drawer. You're all set to go!"

He had a point. They were both a bit offended and just going round in circles here. What did he really want? And more importantly, what the hell did *she* want?

She was so aware of his presence that it hurt. She could smell him, could literally feel his warmth and wanted to touch him. But she had to resist that temptation. She couldn't let herself get involved with him again. It would break her. She had only just made herself strong again, or so she had thought.

Lyle's breath caught. He hadn't thought this through standing so close to her. He just wanted to pull her to him and kiss her to the ground. Maybe then she would finally come to her senses and stop talking about a divorce. His gaze landed on her mouth. His eyes darkened. Mel saw it and avoided him.

"No. Keep your distance." she warned him weakly. She took several steps away from him.

"So that's the reason for the divorce? You can't stand to be near me? Because of Roger? Or someone else?"

He had totally misunderstood her caution. But that was just as well. How could she explain to him that she wanted nothing more than to spend the nights with *him*, and the days. But she couldn't. She didn't have the strength to lose herself in him again. She would never be able to get up again.

His gaze became cool and sobered again. She didn't dare breathe. "I'll be working here for the next few weeks … months, so I can be with you, support you with your business, as your *husband*. At least in public."

Mel was silent. They were not quite the words she had expected. Not at all.

"We only need to show ourselves together among people. We can *spare* ourselves everything else. Going out to eat now and then, here and there. Show ourselves. That's what I expect from our marriage. Is that too much to ask?"

Mel was torn. It sounded doable. After all, in the many months that had passed, they had managed to *be* together but not *live* together. He would surely stay out of her way for most of the time and she could continue her business in peace. How bad could such dinners get? And she'd certainly have to attend a few business dinners too, so at least she'd have company.

If that meant she didn't have to make a decision at this moment, then she was fine with that.

"No." she replied slowly, pausing briefly in her acceptance. "So, as ever. A marriage on paper."

"Or something like that." came his reply. He looked at her bitterly. "In front of others, you'll have to be okay with me getting a little closer."

He stepped closer to her as if to test his statement. She took a faltering breath. Her eyes sparkled with a hot warning. But he overlooked it and would not be stopped.

His fingers tenderly stroked her cheek. Her whole body trembled at his touch. His gaze did not take its eyes off her for a second. She closed her eyes, not trusting herself. How would she react if she looked at him now?

"I can leave you alone if that's what you want." he said softly. He struggled with himself not to lose his own composure. He lifted her chin with his fingers. Her skin was so soft, so hot. He really wanted to burn himself. But only if she wanted it too. Her eyes popped open; panic written in them as well as many other emotions. He couldn't read them.

"Friday is our first dinner. Play businesswoman this week and then I'll see you on Friday." He hesitated another moment. "As my *wife*."

Mel swallowed, ignoring the endless desire burning inside her. She had to keep her head, couldn't allow herself to jump head first into this hopeless relationship. She needed all her strength and senses to run her business and make it a success. She had no time for these games.

She grabbed his hand and pushed it away from her.

"I will be the perfect wife. Don't you worry." Her cold words did not match the heat she felt inside her. But enough for today. He should leave. "You do your thing and I'll do mine. We won't get

in each other's way. Except for my duties of course."
Lyle nodded slightly.
"You can be both. A successful businesswoman and my devoted wife. We don't have to choose."
She laughed lightly. He had chosen his words well.
"I look forward to our dinner on Friday, Melissa McClory." He looked at her again urgently before leaving her flat without further ado.
Melissa grinned. Devoted. Definitely. Not.

~ 112 ~

Melissa should have been exhausted. She should have wanted nothing more than to fall into her bed and sleep. But she was so full of joy and pride that she couldn't help but break into a big smile. What a week it had been. The first five days had been a total success. No question about it. The classes had all been fully booked, the families had all had nothing but positive comments and experiences too. And the children - the children were the best. They had really given their best, had experimented, had dreamt and painted, told and drawn. Their eyes had sparkled, their laughter had brightened every day. Each class had something special about it. All these memories of joy would linger in her heart for a long time. She was already looking forward to next week and the one after that. How many other children and families would she meet and be able to offer them a piece of her art? She was about to find out now.

With the warmest feeling in her stomach and heart, she drove to the restaurant where she'd been told to meet Lyle. He had kept his word, and really left her alone all week. And to be honest, she hadn't had time to think about him much at all. She had known she would see him again soon. That added to her joy. Today she finally saw him again and she could hardly wait to tell him about her week. In principle, she didn't mind playing his wife in front of the other people in the restaurant. Nothing could spoil her mood today. It was the beginning of a new exciting life, and with Lyle at least half by her side. She even dared to dream that she might have the power to make him fall in love with her. Yes then, then she would have *everything* she needed in her life. The children's happiness and her own happiness.

Melissa reminded herself quietly to *calm down*. Let the evening happen first. It will take some time with his affection. Despite all this, she had butterflies in her stomach. She could achieve anything; she was *sure* of it.

She stepped confidently into the noble restaurant. All the years she had lived in this area, she had never seen the inside. Something nagged at her, wanting to tell her that maybe she didn't fit in, in her simple dress, and boring bun in her hair. She ignored the wavering feeling of her self-consciousness and headed for the illuminated bar. Lyle was going to meet her here and show themselves to the public and so she complied. Once they were seated at the table, she wouldn't be the centre of attention. Then her plainness wouldn't stand out as blatantly as it did right here. She saw only beautiful attractive women around her. All of them in the finest of dresses. Their jewellery glittered on their arms and necks. The room was filled with a mixture of fine perfumes and aftershaves. She absorbed the scent as she inhaled deeply.

Don't let it get you down, she told herself. Lyle will be right by your side.

"Melissa, good to see you again."

She looked into Kurt Randall's eyes in surprise. He was not someone she would have expected to see here. He looked a little older than she remembered. Yet dapper in his dark suit. His silver-grey hair cut short and neatly worn. He looked at her kindly, kissed her cheek and smiled. As ever the perfect gentleman.

Mel needed a moment to collect her thoughts. She was a little confused to see him here.

"Kurt. Yes, it's been a while." she finally replied. She hoped her smile didn't show her inner panic that was slowly rising inside her. So, this was their first dinner. Just like *old* times. "I take it your wife is here too."

"Yes, and I'm afraid she hasn't changed."

"That sounds promising."

They both laughed openly. She liked this man. What did he see in that irritating woman, she wondered once again.

Kurt took her gently by the elbow and led her around the magnificent room, past the tables. All eyes were on her and her bland dress and boring appearance. She unconsciously pulled at her jacket to cover herself more. It didn't help.

Mel slowly began to realise what this evening was all about. It was no coincidence to find him here. This dinner had obviously been planned, for all of them together. Why hadn't Lyle told her that up front? Because then she definitely wouldn't have agreed. As you pointed out, he knows you better than you thought.

And too right, she wouldn't have come. She had absolutely no interest in sitting at a table with Angela and listening to her talking down to her and making eyes at Lyle at the same time. *Her* husband.

Damn it, it was too late to turn around and leave. She had to get through it. This was the first and last time she was available for a dinner, she told herself, and truly meant it at that moment.

Then she saw Lyle. He was sitting across the table from Angela, smiling at this beauty. Whatever they were discussing delighted him and he looked stunning. His hair styled yet so wild. His grey suit fitted him like a male model. At that moment she felt great pride and an even greater need to say that he *was* her husband. Jealousy did not agree with her at all. Still, after all these months, it bothered her immensely that he could laugh with Angela and not with her. How could he be so free with her? What did he hate about Mel that he never gave himself like that in her presence?

His eyes met hers and for just a second, time stopped. There were only the two of them in the room. His smile didn't disappear, on the contrary it only deepened and an indescribable feeling came over them both when they saw each other. She returned his gaze. Then the spell was broken when Angela turned to her.

Lyle probably hadn't told her who was coming to dinner either, because she looked just as pissed off as Mel had felt a few minutes ago. At least she has had a little time to prepare herself mentally for this meeting and now she could nod confidently at the beautiful woman. However, that was all she could master at that moment.

Angela still looked amazing. Her sleek long hair lay across her bare shoulders, leaving her back bare and for all to admire and desire. Her gold-coloured dress was a super tight fit. It left no doubt as to what she might or might not be wearing underneath. But her face was cold and definitely not inviting. She did not hide her deep dislike for the younger woman in the slightest.

Melissa took the last two steps towards Lyle, who had to rise so that she could sit next to him on the bench. As he did so, his hands brushed gently over her waist, leaving a hot trail on her body that ate through to her skin. Had he done this on purpose? Was he *testing* how she reacted to him in public? Or had it not been intentional at all?

She took a seat next to him, wishing the evening was already over and yet it hadn't even started.

"Oh, you've found your wife again," came the biting greeting from across the table. Kurt cleared his throat loudly to interrupt his wife, but she was having her fun embarrassing the young woman.

"What would you recommend here?" tried Mel to deflect, steering all her attention to Kurt, who was just as happy to study the menu with her.

"Of course, you have no idea what people eat in our circles."

"Angela!" Kurt was less amused this time and his gaze was cold. He couldn't understand why Mel was such a thorn in his wife's eye.

Melissa searched frantically for some strong answers, but her mind went blank. She also noticed that Lyle did not speak up for her. On the contrary, he sat there drinking his glass of champagne. As if none of this was any of his business. Just *like* old times.

Melissa felt the anger rising inside her. She had had such a great feeling, had been so looking forward to seeing him tonight and now this cold front and avoidance. Hadn't he just been laughing with the unsympathetic woman? About her?

Fortunately, the conversation finally turned to business and Lyle and Kurt discussed the next plans and appointments they had to keep. Angela kept throwing in a word here and there to show who fit in and who didn't.

Melissa was quiet and poked listlessly at her salad. Who ordered bloody salad in one of the best restaurants? She loved her food; she had never been into this green stuff and now all of a sudden, she had ordered *this*? Why the hell? To prove something to this woman. To show that she was trying to lose some weight. To fit *into* this world.

No way. That wasn't her. That was a result of this pretence of a devoted wife who couldn't keep up with her successful husband. That was no longer the case. She *had* outgrown this.

As the waiter cleared the plates away, she ordered herself a dessert. The biggest one on the menu. It was the most delicious thing she had enjoyed in a long time. She felt instantly better. Sugar always helped. Angela just watched her enviously and drank her fourth glass of wine in one go. Her repulsion was becoming more unbearable by the minute.

Melissa just wanted the bill and to say goodbye. To *all* of them.

"You two." she finally began. She had been waiting all evening to get it off her chest. Now, at a guess the alcohol gave her enough courage. "How long are you going to keep up this game?"

Mel stared at her in shock. Lyle gave his wife a warning look.

"Angela, we should pay." Kurt said and waved at the waiter. But his shrewd wife had now tasted blood. The expression of being caught out on Melissa's face was blatant. She wanted to really *crush* the young wife of his to the ground.

"It's all for show. Anyone can see that." Her eyes sputtered hate and envy at the same time. She'd had too much to drink, had too much going for Lyle, and too little interest in Melissa's feelings to stop herself now. "You only married him to get his money. You cold, manipulative brat."

Lyle was a little more supportive this time and rose abruptly.

"Angela! What do you think you're doing? Apologise to Melissa."

But Mel had heard enough. She didn't want an apology, didn't want to hear any more insinuations, true or false. She wanted to be somewhere else, but not here. She was not wanted here. This was not where *she* wanted to be.

She took that opportunity to slide past Lyle and stood up. He stared at her silently, his eyes full of regret and a plea.

Stay, they should tell her. But she shook her head, barely noticeable, and left the room quickly. All eyes were once again on her. She would have liked to run, wanted to get out of this restaurant, just get out. But as heaven would have it, *everywhere* there was someone in the way, there was always an obstacle in front of her and it took her *forever* until she was finally outside, inhaling in the fresh air again. She breathed in the cool air deeply as if she had been suffocated. Her head full of thoughts, her heart heavy. The initial joys and excitements completely forgotten. As if the last six months hadn't even happened, she suddenly felt so help-less and ... alone again.

No, not again. This *had* to end.

She waited impatiently for the valet to finally bring her car around. A car that had brought her nothing but trouble.

"You just run off like that?" she heard *his* voice behind her. She closed her eyes for seconds before turning to face him. She wrapped her thin jacket around her body. She needed more pro-tection from his cold and angry demeanour.

"Dinner was finished." she said just as coldly. She felt inside her-self how she had no mental strength left. Her tiredness made her feel more vulnerable than usual.

"Because of your childish behaviour, you only confirmed her stupid accusations. Mel, we had agreed- "

"My childish behaviour?" she snapped. "All she did *all* night was put me down and you sat there like you were of the same opin-ion! I definitely didn't agree to *that*."

Endlessly irritated by the events of the evening, Lyle ran a hand carelessly through his hair. He had to admit to himself that this evening couldn't have gone worse.

"You know what she is like."

"You didn't even tell me we were meeting them for dinner. Didn't give me a chance to prepare for it."

"You would have refused."

"And rightly so." she agreed. Something was breaking inside her. She couldn't stop it and continue to ignore it. That voice inside her had been screaming the depressing, disappointing truth for so long. Admit it, especially to yourself.

"Lyle .... I come from nothing and I have nothing. All those people in there, they stare at me and they see right away that I still *am* nothing.... That I sold *myself* for your money."

Lyle wanted to interrupt her, wanted to stop her from thinking like that. It was insane! She raised her hands to stop him from coming closer. She wasn't finished yet.

"But you know what the worst part of it all is? I *did*. I *sold* myself. I agreed to this marriage to be financially secured. The thought of never having to worry about how I'm going to pay for my rent or my car or my clothes again, yeah, that had appealed to me. I'm such a hypocrite. Angela is absolutely right ... about *everything*. We can't go on with this act."

She felt sick at this realisation. She hadn't wanted to admit it, had pushed it away again and again. But now it was time to be honest. If she finally realised it, others would see it too, wouldn't they?

"You did*n't* sell yourself." he disagreed. "Melissa?"

He sought her gaze. Didn't know how to say it wasn't like that. But how? What other reasons had there been?

"You and I, we both had had enough of meaningless relation-ships or heartbreak. We *both* chose this marriage. We *were* and *are* both aware of what it brings us. There had *never* been any talk of anything else."

The valet boy pulled her car to the curb and waited patiently for her with the key in his hand.

"Give *us* another chance. Tomorrow? The day after tomorrow? Next week, dinner for two."

Lyle realised in that moment how much he wanted another chance. He couldn't let her go like this.

"I want a divorce." she said instead and got into her car.

~ 113 ~

Melissa ignored everything *unimportant* in her life and threw herself fully into her work. She loved it and her efforts were rewarded every day. She had read several positive comments in newspapers and her programmes were all booked up. She had also not been able to miss the article about the 'Long awaited homecoming' from the successful writer Lyle McClory to his *wife*. But she quickly turned the pages. She worked late into the night. She had so many children and their pictures that she could hardly keep up with writing a quality story for each of them. She found it easy to draw a sketch or a whole picture to go with the stories, but the other way around took a little more time and talent. She would probably have to hire someone to do that task after all. She pushed away the quiet voice nagging at her that Lyle would be the perfect candidate for the job. She was the brush; he was the book. But her pride would not allow her to ask *him*.

On the contrary, she had*n't* wasted a second thinking about him since dinner. And if she did, then only until she had completely distracted herself again. And then again. Her long hours at work ensured that she fell into bed dead tired in the evening and then had no time to think about him and herself for long. Only her dreams she couldn't quite tame, and he kept appearing in them over and over again. Sometimes they ended with the love she wanted so much. Mostly she woke up with a heavy, broken heart.

Once she signed that stupid divorce paper, everything would be *better*. Guaranteed.

Melissa ran down the stairs to wake herself up a bit, lately that was her only exercise which was more than enough for her. Patty would just shake her head and expect her to get up early to go jogging. Instead, she just ran up and down the stairs, hoping it was sufficient for her health.

She jumped the last few steps and walked out of the building in good spirits only to run straight into his arms. His aftershave hit her like a slap in the face. Then his gaze. She was lost.

"Sorry." she managed with difficulty and stepped back again. A week had passed, once again, and yet all the feelings were already raw again.

"I was beginning to think you'd never finish. I was just coming to get you."

Melissa drew her eyebrows together. She was confused. Had she forgotten they had a date?

"Why?"

"The delightful discussion of our marriage calls. Doesn't it?" he said jokingly, but his eyes were cold.

"Is it calling right now, or maybe tomorrow morning?" She was suddenly totally exhausted and didn't know how she would cope with another argument.

"I've been waiting all week. Now."

He had parked just nearby and was literally shoving her into the passenger seat. After a short drive, he pulled over and they were in front of a small, yet fancy restaurant. Melissa stopped in front of the door. She really wasn't dressed for the occasion. She had paint stains on her top and glue and other materials on her black trousers. She was purely not dressed for an outing with this handsome man.

"It does *not* matter how others see you." he said, holding her gaze. "I only see *you*."

Melissa's heart jumped a thousand feet. She didn't know what exactly he was trying to say, didn't know how much she could read into it. But at that moment she loved him even more and her hopes blossomed.

"And the spots of colour on your bottom too." He added softly as he pushed her into the restaurant. She could have sworn she heard his laughter. Her stomach tightened with excitement. She wanted to give him a smile when she saw the couple at the table in front of them.

All joy vanished from her face and she saw that Lyle hadn't expected to see Angela and Kurt here either. Of all places, especially today.

Lyle automatically put his hand around her waist. To hold her or so she wouldn't run away? She wasn't sure. Her head was spinning. She wanted to be invisible.

The other two looked at her in surprise and before she knew what was happening, they were sitting together at one of the smallest tables in this cosy restaurant. What an exciting déjà vu. Melissa could hardly contain her joy.

"Well, this is a surprise," Kurt said kindly. His eyes sparkled, he looked almost relieved to meet them there. It meant he had company and didn't just have to listen to his moody wife. His wife who actually looked *normal* for once. Still in the most beautiful dress and a great hairstyle, of course, and yet a little less styled up and glittery.

Her gaze was condescending as she looked at Mel in front of her. This time Mel stood before her much prouder and taller. The stains on her clothes were from her successful day, from her own company. They were physical signs, proof of the children's joy on her.

"Are you two lost?"

Lyle reached for Mel's hand under the table. She recoiled at first, a gesture so innocent so unexpected on his part. She didn't need to think, she took his hand gratefully. This smallest gesture meant the world to her and gave her the courage to get through this evening together and not let it get her down. She remembered all those stupid rules about not giving each other affection in public. His hand gave her the greatest support.

"I obviously didn't just get my hands dirty at work, I got everything dirty." she joked, smiling bravely.

Kurt returned her good humour immediately and helped her keep the conversation going.

"Your work? I didn't even know you were back at work. Did Lyle let you go?"

"Of course not. She is and always will be my illustrator, for *all* my stories."

"I've started my own business. Melissa's Easy Art Easy Heart." she replied and the glow on her face was genuine. She was happy to talk cheerfully about her ideas. She completely forgot who was sitting right in front of her, so engrossed was she in her answers. It was long overdue to talk about *her* own numerous achievements.

"A troublesome project. Way too much work, way too little profit." Angela put in. She had not yet managed to join in. Now, however, it was about time she added her insulting insights.

"Not a project. A compassionate business." interrupted Lyle this time. He saw out of the corner of his eye that Mel was smiling at him. "Melissa has invested six months in making it all a reality. It's a great success."

"That's why she dumped you? For a few painting lessons?"

Melissa bit her lips. Don't let on. Ignore her. Take a deep breath.

"You're welcome to come by and paint with us sometime. It's good for the soul." she said invitingly. But Angela was obviously not interested in that.

"Nonsense. Just a waste of time and precious utensils go to waste. Who cares what children want to paint? Once again, a totally childish attitude to life."

Lyle was about to jump in and defend her when Melissa continued to speak as well, finally finding her own voice again. *Screw you, bitch.*

"I do care. And a lot more people should care. We can't all go through life as callous and selfish as … some people."

She put down her napkin and rose. Lyle looked at her warningly. Not again, his eyes said. This time, though, there was more in her gaze. She found the strength even to skirt the rules a little herself. She leaned towards him, whispering in his ear.

"I'll be back." And then she did something she never usually did in public, and especially in front of Angela, she kissed him softly on the mouth. The kiss had been breathy, only for a split second, yet long enough for it to relight the fire. Both felt the electricity, both immediately pulled away as if burned. They were not alone.

When she came back, Kurt and Angela had already left. She couldn't say she was disappointed that they hadn't said good-bye to her. She was more than relieved. The evening could be much more pleasant now.

"Did all your acquaintances move here with you?" She tried to sound casual, but it was taking an immense toll on her.

"Kurt and I are working on the next children's series - I need him near me. He was willing to take a holiday here for a while."

"Who else can I expect to see?" she asked bravely, then a little more shyly. "Verona?"

Lyle gritted his teeth for a moment. But he did not let his anger get through. He hesitated, thinking how best to answer.

Mel saw his anger. *Nothing* had changed. She couldn't breathe.

"Verona and Richard have found each other again." He shook his head incomprehensibly, his anger so unbridled. How deep did his feelings run for this impossibly beautiful woman? "With her biography, a few truths were brought to light that helped them put the past behind them and start anew."

His tone was so bitterly cold that Mel sensed how opposed he was to this bond. He had had more feelings for this gorgeous woman after all. Hadn't she known it? She hadn't wanted to admit it. Still couldn't bear it. Jealousy didn't agree with her.

"And that bothers you. Verona and you, you have a -"

"It bothers me because I know what a piece of shit Richard is. After that night, with you and him..."

Lyle clenched his hands into fists, remembering just as she had the moment Richard had assaulted her. If he hadn't come ... Melissa pushed the thoughts far away. For a moment she found it promising that he was angry about *that*, not about losing Verona. But it didn't last long. That night was far from erased from memory. For either of them.

"*Stop.*"

She still couldn't think about that, so instead she steered their conversation to neutral topics. Lyle accepted her wish not to bring it up again.

Like old times, they talked about his work, about hers, not noticing how time flew. Not with one syllable did they talk about .... the divorce.

He quietly drove her back to her car, which she had left at work. They stood there not knowing what to do.

"Mel, I'm so- " he began.

"Thank you." she interrupted him before he could continue. "Today was the first time with your friends that I *didn't* feel alone. Today I was your wife."

She smiled at him. She looked ravishing in that harsh street light. And she was his.

"Come back to the hotel with me."

Everything instantly tightened so strongly that it took her breath away. Everything, really everything, inside her reacted to the thought of being alone with him. To *really* be alone. She felt the same endless desire. Was so close to following him there. But her friend's voice whispered deep inside her. Don't do it. The deeper you will fall and not recover.

"Let us part in peace. Our next argument will come soon enough."

"Melissa - "

She barely shook her head before turning away and getting into her car.

Lyle felt an endless longing inside him that he had never experienced before. What on earth was going on here? Was she still with Roger? Was it jealousy that was leading him here with her?

~ 114 ~

It went perfectly, smoothly, a once in a lifetime experience for everyone. She spent most of her time on her hands and knees with the toddlers, totally immersed in paint and other stuff. Or in front of an easel, giving her teenagers an idea of colours - oil, water, brushstroke, paper or canvas, etc. It was a new world for many, a familiar world for others. Her children all had great talent. She felt honoured to be part of their discovery, their journeys. Some stories were stepping stones to something better. She wanted to show some of them to Lyle and see what he thought.

Since their last meeting, she had a warm feeling in her stomach whenever she thought of him. Secretly, she was waiting for him to appear, to be near her. She couldn't wait to see him again. Alone. Without Angela and Kurt this time. It was becoming more and more unbearable.

Melissa was hanging the various pictures on the drying racks when he entered. At last. Hadn't she wished for it? She looked up briefly and beamed at him. It was impossible for her to react to him in any other way. She was overcome with pride looking at the pictures of her children. She had to share these moments with someone or she would burst with joy.

"Come and have a look!" she urged him. She was so excited and so infectious in her mood that Lyle followed her and looked at everything. He only now realised all she had achieved and how much it meant to her. These countless pictures were mostly nothing more than stick men or a few flowers, but to her they were the beginning of a story. The beginning of a dream. He saw it in her big brown eyes, how she was literally absorbed in her work. She was *happy* here. She would probably never come home with him again. Not voluntarily.

"And the stories! Lyle, such imagination and ideas."

He could have listened to her for hours. Didn't want to lose this moment with her. The next argument came soon enough, her words ringing in his ears.

After quite a while she finished in the room and he followed her into her office. More pictures and materials were piled up there, all carefully sorted and labelled. She was impressed herself, how she managed to get it all organised and was still standing upright, smiling.

"What brings you to me?" Her question had been meant to sound light. The mood was not supposed to change to cold utterances and remarks, as it so often, so quickly did.

"I need ... your company." he answered directly. There was no point in beating about the bush. She was still delighted and upbeat from her successes, best to convince her now.

"Oh, I see. My duties as your wife." she clarified. Immediately she felt slight panic as to why exactly he needed her.

"On Saturday we are invited to a charity event. As you know, I've been donating the proceeds of my children's books to all sorts of children's charities for years. They want to use my name to raise more money."

Mel swallowed dryly. She was crazy proud of his work and found it heart-warming that he thought about children as much as she did. But an event like this meant many, many people. Many, many questions and *thousands* of eyes on them as a couple. On her as his wife...

"I've had enough of this world. That's why I left." she said honestly. The thought alone worried her.

"But I will be there *with* you. By your side."

"Not really. You're there to show your face to as many people as possible, not to be with *me*."

"That's just how these fundraisers work." He defended himself cautiously.

"I don't want that anymore. Everyone looks at me and knows I

don't belong in this world. And I know it too. I'm sorry."
Lyle did not accept her rejection. He saw no other way but to repeat the rules again. How else could he persuade her to stand by his side?
"You have no choice, Mel."
Her gaze turned dark and cold. She drew her eyebrows together in annoyance. This guy. Hadn't they been getting along just fine a moment ago? Hadn't she *wanted* to see him again because their last night together had been so ...real? Just why again?
"People have already noticed that you weren't there on the book tour. Now I've come all this way here to see you. Showed my face at your opening evening. Now it's your turn to be my wife."
"I didn't ask you to follow me here." she interjected. She couldn't believe he was about to come at her with the contract.
"It's only a matter of time before someone tells my sister and then we could lose everything."
"You waited six months, why only now?"
Lyle looked at her intensely. At that moment he had no idea how he had lasted even a day without her.
"I wanted to give you time to get over this crush with Roger. I couldn't bear the thought of you and him. I threw myself into the reading promotion to distract myself. That's enough now. Six months will have to be enough for you and him. Now you're *my* wife again, fully and completely. This is *our* world."
"No, I'm not following you back into your world. I want to offer my children everything, more. I need my time and energy here. I don't want to waste any of that on these people."
She did not react to his insinuation about her relationship with Roger. She did not hear how he had found it unbearable. She had to shield herself. Everything she said was the utmost truth. She could no longer reconcile herself to constantly maintaining an act *and* giving everything to her company. Why did he have to corner her like this?
"Your ideas are unique and truly beneficial to all the children you are targeting." Lyle sounded sincere, but his tone was neutral and forceful. He had no choice but to bring the purest truth

to her as well. "But this business, with your employees and your expenses, is not going to make you any money. It will always *cost* you more money than you gain because it is for the children and not profit... If we *lose* the inheritance ...... your business will go under just the same."

Melissa felt an icy chill run down her spine. She wanted to be angry and throw him out. She never wanted to see him again and just scream. But she heard these facts, heard the truth, and she knew, deeply distressed, that he was right. Without the income of the inheritance, she had no chance of survival. She might be able to stay afloat for six months, but the salaries of her employees were high. The lease costs were elaborate, the maintenance costs ... her own rent ... her food ... she paid herself no salary, so would own nothing. The materials cost more and more each month, the more interest she got. And she wanted to give all the children a chance to come here and participate, whether they had money or not.

She needed this marriage. She needed the money. Damn, what had happened to her?

"Okay."

"Okay what?"

"I'll go with you to this event."

"*And* to any other public meetings we should attend together."

Melissa nodded weakly. Her joy and cheerfulness from earlier had faded.

He hesitated again. He was sorry that she suddenly looked so broken. He felt the urge to pull her into his arms and hold her. But he did not trust himself. A hug might not be enough. He didn't want to overstep his boundaries. Unless she was willing for him to do so.

"See you on Saturday." He made to leave, turning to her once more. "And just so you know. It was six months and fifteen days that I had to wait."

She looked up, confused as to why he had counted the time accurately. And she remembered his fantasies and misconceptions of what had been going on between her and Roger. His

words came through to her again.
"And just so you know. Nothing ever happened with Roger."
His expression was unreadable, but she thought he looked a lit-
tle relieved, maybe even glad. She should have told him this a
long time ago. At last, it was out.
"Then I can finally seduce you again."
And with that he left her standing there.

~ 115 ~

Mel winced when the doorbell rang. She had just made herself comfortable, on her living room floor, surrounded by all kinds of pictures and stories. She wanted to go over them again, look at them once more and give each one her best attention. It was getting late; she wasn't expecting anyone.

She picked up the handset, and heard Lyle's voice. She pressed the button to open the front door for him. She looked down at herself for a moment. She didn't have time to do anything about her homely look. Her hair was all wild, most strands had already escaped from her bun, and her face was pure of anything fake. As always, she saw herself as not worthy of his attention.

And he looked simply brilliant. His tight jeans fitted him too well, his shirt looked soft and inviting. His hair lay wildly on his head, but not as messy as hers.

He had several hangers and other things in his hand. He did not hesitate for a moment and entered. He saw the many papers and pens and so on on the floor.

"Shall we go to your bedroom?" He nodded at the things in his hands and she agreed, caught off guard.

She ignored the sudden tingle in her stomach when she saw him in front of her *bed*. He put the things down and turned to face her.

The room suddenly seemed far too small and Melissa was very, very aware of his presence immediately within a moment's reach. She swallowed dryly and tried not to let her mind wander.

"I asked Elsa to send you your clothes. For our outings together." he explained deadpan, glancing at her.

"I'm sure she was thrilled." That definitely didn't help her strained relationship with the housekeeper.

She propped her arms on her hips in a huff, the thin fabric of her worn t-shirt stretching across her breasts. It did not go unnoticed by Lyle.

"Maybe you'll feel more like you're part of this circle, too, with your clothes on," he said distractedly. Their bodies so close, it was unbearable.

Melissa opened some of the covers. Countless memories came flooding back, loneliness and emptiness. Sadness. She immediately stepped back again.

"Is my usual dress code not appropriate for our play?" She knew the answer herself, but was still a little disappointed that he wanted to force these things on her again. Did that come with a visit to the hairdresser or a few lessons on how to behave among stuck up people?

"What else doesn't suit you anymore? My hair? My scent?"

Lyle's eyes sparkled at her remark. She had no idea how ecstasizing he found her right now. And her scent... he could never forget it and it drove him crazy not to be able to press his face into her neck and just breathe it in, deeply, fully.

"I would prefer it if you wore nothing at all. And that we didn't have to go out."

Mel stared at him. Served her right with her stupid questioning. His gaze was full on and her body immediately responded to him with hot desire. She had to stay strong, however, the attraction between them seemed to double with every second. So, he had meant it, he wanted to seduce her again. Did she want that too?

Hell *yes*.

"Do you want something to drink?" In her panic, she looked for an excuse to get out of his presence, out of this room. His eyes didn't leave her out of his sight for one moment. She felt trapped, afraid that she was not up to his expectations.

"No." he said coolly, with his intense gaze still on her face. He took a step towards her. Her knees went weak, her heart pounding in her throat. He slowly raised his hand and touched the loose strands of hair that curled around her face. One by one, so careful not to accidentally touch her skin. His breath was shallow. His gaze only on her. She could hardly bear it. Waiting for him to pull her into his arms and make love to her right here and now. She wouldn't hesitate for a second. Her body was more than willing and her mind was quiet for once.

"Wear what you wish. As long as you're by my side, I don't care what."

He let go of her hair, and moved away from her again. Mel felt a thousand emotions, but the strongest was disappointment. Hadn't he wanted the same thing? Felt the same desire inside him as she did? Why hadn't he kissed her? Was he maybe no longer interested in the side of her marriage? Was he just trying to play on her emotions?

How the hell did he want to seduce her then, if not here in her bedroom, in the middle of the night, alone?

"See you tomorrow night. We'll pick you up." He looked her straight in the eye, no emotion, nothing. "I added another dress. Happy anniversary, Melissa."

She watched him leave, with a bitter look on her face. Their wedding anniversary and such an insult. Didn't people usually celebrate it differently?

He just left her standing there. It had only been two years. There was simply nothing to celebrate.

~ 116 ~

Melissa stood undecided in front of her wardrobe. Last week she had only owned one elegant dress, today she had so many that she had already lost count. Every single one was a gem, looked enchanting and yet she wasn't sure if she should wear it. She was not as thin as the others, was not as glamorous as Angela. She wore little, if any, make-up and she had no idea what could be done with her long brown hair. She didn't like nail polish and jewellery, hadn't worn it for years either. She was so poop-normal it hurt.

Some defiance in her wanted to put on jeans and a T-shirt to see what his reaction would really be if she showed up like that. And then again, she remembered their agreement. After all, it was for the sake of her business, not just for him. She had to give in a little so that they could both benefit.

And the anniversary present was ... perfect. He had chosen it well, if indeed it had been Lyle himself who had bought it and not Joyce or Elsa even. The right colour, shape, material. It felt just right. She had to wear it, as much as she resisted to start with. A dark dress, with purple flowers that highlighted her top and added some colour to the long skirt. The little glittering stones sparkled in the light, with every movement. Even with the straps, she felt very naked on her upper body. But as if he had guessed her insecurities, it had a small, thin cardigan with it, which helped her feel more comfortable immediately. After all, he knew her so well. She wore her hair in a tight, neat bun, as always, where she could put almost all her hair, except, as ever, those unruly strands. She even put on some mascara. A light touch of pink on her lips and she looked contentedly into the mirror. That should do it.

The car arrived on time. She struggled to walk in those uncomfortable shoes. That was something else she hadn't missed in the last few months.

Lyle was already sitting in the car. One look and her heart leapt into her throat. My goodness again, he looked excitingly hot. And this was *her* husband.

His look didn't reveal whether he liked her or not. He was silent all the way to the theatre where the charity event was to be held. It was swarming with people as they got out of the car. Everyone had dressed in their best and fanciest clothes and Mel was glad at that moment that Lyle had provided her with this dress and all the others. Otherwise, she would never have fit in here.

He sensed her restlessness. He himself was a little nervous about how the evening would go. They were to be seen here as a *married* couple. Had to finally show the public again that their marriage was incredibly strong and not at all breaking up. They had to put to rest any rumours that he or she was having an affair. He was strangely impatient, wanting to get it over with. But he was worried that Mel would resist being near him. He held her back a little before they stepped into the large, festive hall.

"Mel, you are here as my wife." he reminded her. His gaze was insistent, almost a little threatening. His words irritated her to no end. She hadn't forgotten her bloody duties. Never before had he found it necessary to point this out to her.

Her eyes sparkled cold fire. She would not fail him, didn't he know?

She placed the flat of her hand on his cheek, felt his warm skin beneath her fingers. She gently ran her thumb over his lips, biting hers.

"And you as my husband." She whispered back, giving him a hint of a kiss on the lips. Her breath came only haltingly and her stomach tightened convulsively. She had wanted to teach him a lesson, had wanted to tease him convincingly and coolly. Stupidly, her own body had been far from immune to her actions.

The action had almost backfired. His gaze darkened immediately and his hand grasped hers.

She didn't know what he was up to, but she told herself later that he had felt the same way she had at that moment. Racing hearts, hot desire and incomprehensible passion. But alas, the moment was interrupted and the evening began.

Melissa smiled throughout, staying by his side as he made his rounds. She felt a strange sensation every time he introduced her as his 'beautiful' or 'gorgeous' wife. She found it insanely arousing to see all the women looking at him, yet he kept referring them to his wife. Now and then their elbows touched, sometimes he even took her hand and kissed it gently. Again and again, he put his arm around her waist. It was almost unbearable how close he was to her and yet he was not. He showed more than affection, broke all sorts of institutional rules. Drove her crazy. Thoughts of the kiss, his lips and his reaction still floated in her mind. She wanted to do it again, but couldn't find the opportunity or even the courage to dare to do it in front of everyone. The evening went on *and on*.

During the meal, they sat a little apart from each other. That gave her a moment to calm down again, to get her sexual desire back under control. He had a speech or two to make, and he gave out several awards. She was still smiling, talking to all sorts of people. All were very interested in his book and the children's series, in his life, some were also impressed by her own company. But only for a few seconds before they started talking about him again. She was *just* his wife here. Nothing more, actually much less. Did he see her the same way as the others here? In fact, just an accessory at his side? Or did he believe in her company? Was she a woman in his eyes or just his wife?

Mel picked up the champagne glass to toast with the others. She had made it through the evening so far. A small sip of alcohol would probably give her the remaining strength to talk to the last few people and rave to them about her successful husband. She did what was expected of her, but could not refrain from mentioning her own company again and again. Someone will remember and pass it on.

Finally, Lyle was back at her side, looking pleased and still totally gorgeous. She wanted to rip his clothes *off*.

Damn, she had drunk a whole glass of champagne. Her thoughts were not all that clear as they normally were. She felt the heat rising in her ears, but also in her stomach. She had to keep her distance as far as possible, otherwise she couldn't guarantee anything.

In the car, she immediately took off her shoes, and massaged her feet. That had been torture. She wondered if she could sneak loafers in under a long dress next time. She giggled a little to herself.

Lyle looked at her strangely.

"Why are you laughing?" he asked, puzzled. Her eyes sparkled. She looked *adorable*.

"The dress was perfect. But I want comfortable shoes for our next wedding anniversary." she said funny, not noticing his look. Also not realising, what she said. So there will be another anniversary?

Melissa leaned back in the seat, stuck her feet out and nimbly undid her hair. She tousled it a little, easing the tension on her scalp. Now just to get rid of this dress.

He watched her speechlessly. Didn't she know what she was doing to him here? How arousing her actions were?

Mel turned her head in his direction and froze. He had only been watching her, with a look she couldn't interpret. Her hair fell softly around her face. Her gaze moved from his eyes to his lips. "Melissa."

She had unbuckled her seatbelt and was in his arms. Without hesitation, he ran his hands through her hair and pulled her head towards him as far as it would go. His mouth greedily sought hers. She returned his kiss only too willingly, opening herself to him without hesitation. A deep sigh escaped her as she felt his hands teasingly make their way down her back, to her bottom. His grip tightened and she responded. She ran her hands through his hair, following the pressure of his hands, and leaned towards his kiss, unable to be close enough to him.

The car had long since stopped in front of her flat, but they had not noticed as much.

Only with great effort and some sort of willpower did he let go of her. Her hair fell in her face, his hands on her neck. Her lips shone with moisture. He struggled with himself not to assault her lips again. Her breath was staggered, her eyes so dark.

He fought the passion. Couldn't give in to his lust here and now. Didn't want to.

"I want all of you." His voice was so deep and so arousing. "But not like this. I want to be the only one to take your senses away, not the alcohol."

Mel pulled away from him. Disappointed, offended and *relieved*. She had almost made a big mistake. Something she had sworn not to do again. She knew how much he could hurt her. She should be glad; he made this decision. So why did she feel angry? Why was she bitterly disappointed that he *could* say no? And why, at the same time, was she immensely relieved that he had kept his head?

She was looking for her shoes and about to get out of the car when his hand stopped her once more.

"Dream of me." he said and gave her one last goodbye kiss that made her giddy.

There was no end to the night. Had she made a complete fool of herself?

~ 117 ~

The next week came and Melissa could put the weekend behind her. It was better not to think about it any further. He had made the right decision; it was much better that way. Once she gave herself to him again, everything would only get much more complicated. She didn't have time for that. She had all her hands and evenings full with giving her children what she had promised in her advertisements. Unfortunately, she did not find enough hours in the day to do it all herself. The pressure increased.

"Why didn't you ask me?" Lyle threw a newspaper in her direction. She was currently kneeling on the floor of her office, in front of the many pictures, and hadn't seen or heard him come in. It surprised her for a moment that her senses hadn't noticed him at all. Perhaps this constant pressure and challenge to be the best was really doing her life good.

She immediately suppressed the joy that wanted to rise in her. She only had a few minutes before her next class started. She was not prepared for a conversation with him now, *never* really was.

She glanced at the lines in the newspaper at her feet, which he had underlined quite starkly and in neon colours. Whatever it said had *really* pissed him off. She immediately recognised what it was about. Her own ad, where she was looking for a qualified writer who could write children's stories to a wide variety of illustrations, sometimes on the spot.

Of course, Lyle was the perfect candidate for that. She had been more than aware of that.

She straightened up. Her clothes were full of brightly coloured patches of paint and her hair had already come loose from her hairstyle again. He wanted to brush the curls behind her ears.

Melissa looked at her watch for a moment. Then back at Lyle. *Oh*, was all she could think.

"You're overqualified."

Lyle shook his head sourly. It annoyed him so *bloody* much that she hadn't thought of him.

"Really? That's your excuse?" His voice sounded cold. His eyes were cool. "I could write your stories for no pay and attract more people to join in in the first place."

"That's exactly what I don't want," she interrupted him immediately. "This is my business. *Mine.* I don't want to use your name. I want all people to see that *I* am worthy too. Not just you."

Lyle stared at her in surprise.

"Of course, you are. You're an excellent illustrator. You've won awards for your drawings."

"For your books!" She shook her head. She was serious. She was going to make it on her own. "No one took me seriously when we were at your event on Saturday. They only saw your *wife*, not *me*."

"You're my wife, too," he said. "The rest will come with time."

"My business remains mine. I can do it alone. Maybe then you can accept me for more than just Melissa McClory."

"I know you can do this. I was just trying to *help* you out."

She bit her lip. Should she give him a chance? Should she allow him to be a permanent part of her business? No, certainly not. Not yet.

Lyle was with her in one step. His hands on her shoulders, his gaze serious.

She looked into his eyes, lost in the blue. He was so close to her again. She couldn't form a clear thought.

"Stop that." he said softly.

"Stop what?" She stared at him, puzzled.

"This." He stroked her lips gently. His gaze darkened at his touch. He had wanted to stay away from her. Had wanted to wait until she made the first move, but he was only a man. *Her* man. "You do that every time you worry too much."

Mel wasn't even aware of it. But what she did know was his body so awfully close to hers. His fingers on her lips. His aftershave.

"I don't want you to work here." she finally repeated her decision, feeling him pull away from her. He gritted his teeth. He was ready to leave again, but she grabbed his arm. "Because ... Because I can't think straight around you. Alcohol or no alcohol."

Lyle heard her words and responded as his emotions would. He framed her face with his hands and brought his lips down hard on hers. The kiss was overwhelmingly beautiful, unbridled, insistent. She was only too ready to meet the same desire and Lyle felt it instantly. She had to cling to him or her knees wouldn't have supported her. It was mind-blowingly exciting. In any case, she couldn't think anymore, just wanted to act, react.

"Melissa, the next -" Her co-worker stopped awkwardly in mid-sentence. Seeing the two of them in such an embrace was a surprise. She felt the electricity between them from where she was standing.

Melissa stepped back and lowered her head. It took her a few seconds to steady her breathing.

"Yes, thank you. I'm coming."

Lyle smirked at her. He had the same problem, but her employee couldn't see his face.

"We still have to finish this."

Melissa felt her cheeks flush and her ears glow. She had to have desire written all over her face. She ran a hand hastily through her hair, achieving nothing.

"I don't know if that is a good idea."

"Definitely not, but it will feel good."

Mel looked after him. She agreed with him completely.

~ 118 ~

Melissa laughed friendly. Joshua Gibbons was honest, confident and incredibly talented. He would be a perfect fit for her company. He had just the right qualifications, an avid interest in children and he was willing to work for a relatively low wage. She couldn't believe her luck.

Above all, he was helpful and always in a good mood. The early days meant many long hours, and Joshua was always there to help out in the evenings, turning the pictures into short stories in his own words. After a week or so they had soon managed to catch up with all the pictures. Even if they worked late into the night.

"What time is your husband expecting you home?" he asked curiously. He brushed a curl behind his ear that had slipped out of his ponytail. She felt his pain.

Melissa didn't know how to answer his questions at first. She didn't necessarily want to lie, but the truth didn't work either. In all those days, Lyle hadn't shown up at all, which was just as well, she reminded herself. Her staff assumed he had his hands full with his new book. However, during the hours after work, it was a bit more obvious that she didn't rush home to him then.

"There is less time for us during the week, as you can see for yourself. We always keep the weekend free." That was half the truth. She expected to have to go to some event every Saturday. But even that had been limited so far. It almost felt to her like he'd been avoiding her since the last time they'd met. Since their kiss. *The* kiss. Where they had both allowed themselves too much. Or just her? Hadn't he immediately agreed that it would be a mistake to give in to that passion? Yes, he had. So had *she*.

A deep tug in her stomach told her that even today she was not immune to it. Just the thought of it, of *him*, triggered deep desire in her. She had to fight it somehow. Somehow get it *out* of her so that she could concentrate fully on her work again. *Damn it.*

From then on, they only talked about the pictures and tried to find the best and most interesting ones together. This work brought them pretty close together. All the better that he was such a likeable young man. They didn't even notice the time go by.

"Melissa."

She stood shoulder to shoulder next to an attractive young man. He could not believe his eyes. Only just about he managed to contain his anger.

She turned to him and could not suppress a smile. This surprised him instantly, but he held on to his discomfort.

"Lyle. We were just talking about you." she said kindly, nodding at Joshua, who now turned to face him as well. His gaze was open and he held out his hand confidently.

"Mr McClory, nice to meet you. I'm Josh." He seemed sincere, and yet he didn't like this man near Mel at all. He accepted his hand, but nothing more.

"A moment alone... darling."

Mel heard the tense tone in his voice. She followed him into one of the classrooms where he firmly closed the door.

"Who the hell is that?"

"My new writer. Joshua, he's been working here for a while and he's -"

"Did you have to pick the most attractive man for the job?" he interrupted her abruptly. He had no interest in hearing what it was that Josh had or hadn't done.

She tilted her head and narrowed her eyes slightly.

"Are you jealous?"

"Of course, I'm not. Our marriage would have to be real for that to happen." His cruel words escaped him before he could stop himself and Mel's smile faded. She hadn't expected this ice-cold and honest answer. What had she wanted to hear? *You stupid cow*, of course not - he would have to have feelings for her for that.

She was instantly disillusioned and *pissed off*.

"Then why do you care what he looks like?"

"It's what kind of impression other people get of you. You're hanging out here *alone*, late at night. That kind of thing gets around. And hurts our *reputation*."

Mel gritted her teeth, his argument made sense and she could understand it, but she didn't want to agree with him at all right now. He'd better not dare tell her who she could and couldn't hire, depending on their sex and degree of attractiveness. What was he suggesting?

"You're the one who hasn't been in touch for days. People notice *that* just as much."

He gave her a cold look. It had taken everything he had in him to avoid her. Especially since their last encounter. Since *the* kiss.

"That was the deal. I was supposed to leave you alone." he reminded her. "But that's not to say you can then go off and have fun with others."

Melissa shook her head. He was incorrigible. She had had enough.

"Maybe you should call or be in touch. Then you would know that we have been given the opportunity to get our first stories and illustrations published at the end of this month. Joshua has it all lined up. That's why we're working day and night to get everything ready." She was so angry and also so disappointed that he never cared about her success, never asked how it was going or how she felt about it. All he could do was remind her of her stupid contract every time. She knew all the rules inside out. "Maybe you should care a little more about your *wife* after all."

Lyle returned her anger. His temper was shot. She was driving him absolutely crazy. Her, in her motley dirty T-shirt and tight leggings.

He narrowed his eyes.

"What is it then? Do you want me to stay away or not?" He walked towards her. She looked at him in shock but also excitement. Her whole body screamed Take me. Her mind said, Go away. She stepped back until her back was to the door.
"You want me to treat you like my wife or not?" He was now directly in front of her. Only inches with his face separated from hers. Her heart raced; her breath caught. "It's a mistake or not?"
Mel didn't have the chance to answer as he covered her mouth with his. It was a cold, hard kiss. It was possessive and compelling. She braced her hands against his chest to push him off her. To push him away. She didn't want his anger, didn't want this man who was holding her right now. This *really* was a mistake.
She pushed him off her. Her knees trembled; her heart bled.
"Stay away from me." she said directly and meant it. "I won't hurt your reputation, don't you worry. But I don't want any more."
She felt those traitorous tears threatening to well up and promptly turned away from him to get out of the classroom. She didn't cry anymore, wouldn't start because of him.
Joshua was still working, pretending not to notice her sad face. He kept silent and she thanked him inwardly for it.

~ 119 ~

The days went by. If she had assumed that she would be needed at least weekly for her services, she'd be wrong. If she had assumed, she would see him for his birthday, she'd be disappointed. He didn't seem to need her. Left her to do her work. Stayed away from her. She was sure it was for the best. And yet it gnawed at her that he had followed her here into her life and not shown himself. What had been the point of it all? They could have played out this fake marriage at a distance. Why did he first have to stir up her feelings and fears all over again to then leave her standing alone? How could he distract her with his absence more than it seemed possible? She had to mend her ways, curb her thoughts. It couldn't go on like this.

They had just said goodbye to the last of the children and were getting ready to tidy everything up again. A few of her employees helped her out. Among them was Allison, or Ally, the cheerful twenty-year-old who was really a gem when it came to children. She was so full of energy and had a blooming, enchanting imagination. She brought so many children out of their shell. Her classes were always very successful. If a bit noisy and really messy. You had to spend a little longer to put everything back together. She was also a bit wasteful when it came to the materials. Melissa would have to address that with her sometime.

"And I've never painted a rosemary beetle myself before, let alone heard of them. The children were fascinated by the different ways we could depict it. And Matthew had the cutest idea of a story ..."

Mel smiled as she listened to the young woman. It pleased her immensely that these classes not only sparked fun and interest in the children, but also in her staff. She had truly been very lucky in the people she had found and fulfilled her long-awaited dream with her. The other two members of staff had also proved how talented and enthusiastic they were at what they did here. It warmed her heart. The first few months had now passed and were going extremely well.

"Is your husband coming to our party on Saturday?"

Melissa looked at her in surprise. She had suddenly changed the subject without Mel noticing. Her automatic reply almost slipped out before she remembered her contract and nodded.

"Yes, he will be there. He wouldn't miss this opportunity." she lied, not having asked him yet and not really intending to either. He knew nothing of her successes so far, or any of her small achievements. The party on Saturday was only supposed to be for her company, nothing special. If he did come, it would be all about him again. She really wanted to avoid that. Maybe she would ask him to just not be himself for once....

Mel waited until everyone had gone home before she plucked up the courage to call him. She assumed he was in his hotel room. Or where was he hanging out all this time? Was he keeping to their agreement, like she was? Or was he allowed to taint their reputation and their marriage?

Don't think about it, she admonished herself, and dialled his number.

"Yes?" came his cold, impatient voice on the other end. At least he was where he was supposed to be.

"Lyle, it's me...erm...Mel." she faltered. She suddenly didn't know what to say exactly.

"My wife." he finally added. She could have sworn there was a smile behind his words.

"I need you to be my husband. I mean, your services. Erm I ... we ... So -" She was totally overwhelmed as to how she could possibly ask for his services. He did so all the time of her and she couldn't find the right words. She felt her ears burning. She couldn't have embarrassed herself any more.

"Tonight?" he joked. He sounded strangely enticing on the phone. He was obviously in a good mood. She would be only too happy to be in the hotel room with him when he was like this.
"Would you come?"
Mel.
She cleared her throat and started again. She just had to ignore his laughter. And the hot lust that overcame her in one fell swoop. Even the thought of it was unbearable. Remember his aversion, the last kiss, not the *other* kiss. It didn't help. Her head was spinning.
"We made it into the local papers and signed a contract to publish a volume of pictures and stories every month. We're going to celebrate that on Saturday. You should be there. As my husband, but not as an author."
There was silence at the other end. She couldn't see what look was on his face. She had to make sure he knew his role and that he wasn't trying to blind the others with his fame. It was about *her* success, *her* business. Nothing else.
"Lyle?" she asked cautiously. "I wouldn't ask you to come, but there will be other couples there and some important people from the city."
"Of course. I'll go with you."
Melissa was relieved. She had feared that her request had offended him again. She didn't want to upset him. It was so much more exciting when he was friendly like he was now. And so open.
"Lyle? Shall we go?"
Mel's words caught in her throat. She hadn't been talking. He wasn't alone. Her heart broke in two. Was that why he had been in such a good mood? Who was *she*?
"I've changed my mind. It's better if you don't come."
Insurmountable panic caused her to hang up just like that, without asking who it was and what she was doing there. She couldn't hear the answer, didn't want to admit it. She suddenly felt betrayed, and she felt sick. Had she finally caught him in the act? Was this exactly what he had always done, every time he

had stayed away from her for days and nights? *Of course* it was! she persuaded herself. What other man could live for months without a woman? How could she have been so *naïve*? It wasn't a real marriage, no hope of anything anymore. When the hell would she finally realise that?

Stop loving him. Stop dreaming already.

Melissa furiously ran her fingers through her hair. She needed to distract herself. She had to clear her head. The only thing that helped was exercise. All too rarely had she voluntarily thought of going jogging before. But today was an exception.

Her body was screaming. Her legs were crying. She wanted to cry too, but she kept running and running. She couldn't go back to the flat. Not yet. Her emotions were still too raw. She had to run herself all out so she could just fall into bed. She hated it and yet it did her good.

The last few steps were hard. She had pushed too hard, she barely made it back to her block of flats. And saw Lyle sitting on the stairs outside the door. He looked unhappy.

Great, she didn't have enough of her strength left for that now. She fought her wobbly legs and climbed the steps, past him.

"I've been waiting for ages."

"You might as well leave straightaway." she said snappishly and went inside. He jumped up so the door wouldn't slam in the lock and made after her.

Once inside her flat, she looked straight at him, her arms on her hips. Her eyes were ice cold.

"Do you have anything to say to me? Maybe apologise? Or why are you here?"

Lyle had expected her anger. He himself had grown angrier and angrier as he had waited outside for her for an hour, not knowing where the hell she might be.

"I don't need to apologise for anything."

"You arrogant, disloyal, despicable man. You with your double standards." Oh she was beside herself with rage. Where she still found the strength to stand upright, she didn't know. Nor did she care at that moment what she looked like.

"You're completely barking up the wrong tree. Mel - "

"You keep telling me something about keeping your reputation and playing the perfect couple in front of others. Don't hang out with good-looking men. And you? Why can you go behind my back whenever and wherever you want? Over and over again?"

The problem with her anger was that she couldn't contain it. She felt her emotions totally all over the place and she needed to get out of this situation as quickly as possible before she gave away too much what really bugged her.

She tried to walk past him, but he held her by the arm. His gaze serious and holding a hundred questions.

"Don't touch me!" she pleaded, pulling away from his grip. He stood there helplessly. His anger was gone. He wanted to pull her into his arms and hold her. He was confused by his own emotions. Seeing her like this surprised him. Had she really cared when he was *not* with her? Didn't she know how wrong she was?

"Melissa." he began cautiously, but she just shook her head.

"I don't want to hear it." She couldn't bear the truth. She just wanted to get away from him, away from this situation. She could still hear that voice in her head, over and over. She had lived so easily in this oblivion. Had kept telling herself that everything was fine. But now she had heard the other voice. It had been real, not dreamed. Now she knew. She felt sick.

Mel went into the kitchen to get herself something to drink. Her hands were shaking. Her legs were tired.

Lyle watched her. He was searching for the right words for her to hear.

"I don't have double standards, Mel. You hung up so fast I couldn't tell you that."

She stared at his face in disbelief. Her stupid *heart* believed everything. Her mind strongly refused. Why else would he have come all this way and waited for you if what he was saying now wasn't true? Because he wants to keep his inheritance. He would say anything to keep this parade going!

"Now you've said it. Fine." she replied coldly. She saw him clench his hands.

"You're driving me crazy."

"Speak for yourself!" she replied just as desperately. And they both looked into each other's eyes. He dared not approach her, though everything in him demanded it. She looked infinitely tired.

"I will go with you on Saturday. I will do anything you ask of me."

Mel didn't respond to his words. Wanted to be alone to process the evening. Maybe tomorrow she would have the wisdom to interpret everything correctly and move on with this marriage. Now, though, it wasn't a good idea to add anything else to it.

"I want to do everything with you. Everything. But only if you want it too."

With those words, he left her flat. She stood there, her whole body willingly responding to his invitation.

~ 120 ~

Today was the day. Another performance. There was no prize to be won. And yet everything depended on being convincing. The future of her business depended on it.

Mel chose one of *his* dresses. The weather had been a bit unpredictable lately. Sometimes there was rain, sometimes sunshine. For tonight, a short dress with thin tights would surely suffice. She hoped that the new flat shoes she had bought would not cause her any problems. The dress felt really good against her skin. It covered her well enough that she wasn't constantly tugging at herself or was conscious of her cleavage. The silky fabric protected her completely. Her arms were bare. As always, she wore her hair in a tight bun. It was a business party, after all. She didn't want to give anyone the wrong impression, especially Lyle.

They hadn't spoken a word to each other since that evening. She had thought about it almost every day, though. And believed him. It was as simple as that. All he had to do was say one or two things and she was on fire. He had no double standards and he wanted to do everything with her. That was all she remembered now. She had repressed everything else. It was just as well, because today she wasn't going to let it spoil her mood. Today her achievements were being celebrated. For the first time, she was the centre of attention, not just him. Today she was excited, like a little child.

The first issue of the selected pictures had come out yesterday and she loved it. Joshua was really talented and had given the children his best. The pictures had been well reproduced. It was a little masterpiece; she was sure they would all be proud. A couple of parents had already called to thank her. She was almost bursting with joy.

And that's how she approached Lyle. A joyful glow on her face, her eyes sparkled.

He had been waiting for her outside the hall. He too looked amazing in his dinner jacket. No matter how many times she had seen him dressed so smartly, it hit her like a blow every time, what a stunning man he was. Her husband.

He held out his arm for her to take. Her scent was beguiling. He wanted nothing more than to turn back with her and push her into a dark corner and be alone with her. Instead, he walked here beside her, silent and aroused.

The evening went flawlessly. Melissa was completely in her element. She laughed and raved. And people responded to her passion and joy in the same way. They congratulated her for her great collaboration with the arts. It was a great event. Lyle enjoyed watching her.

Every now and then their eyes met. Then he felt her warmth too and it hit him like a bolt of lightning every time she kept her smile even as she looked at him.

Lyle couldn't help it and stepped up to her side. She was chatting with Joshua, who was just as delighted with their achievements as she was. They laughed together and Lyle felt a little jealousy.

"Lyle." she said as he stepped closer, still that gleam in her eye. "You know it was all Joshua's idea to commission the bookshops. It's a great idea."

Lyle just nodded and then looked back at his wife. She was simply beautiful. He leaned in and kissed her on the lips. Only briefly, only fleetingly, and yet the gesture was enough to unsettle her. Her whole body responded to him, so quickly that it took her breath away.

"I'm glad." he said weakly, his gaze captivating hers. They didn't move.

Joshua apologised, feeling awkward, seeing them both like this in front of him. He was clearly not needed here.

"Am I behaving properly?" he asked quietly.

Mel turned to face him properly now. Her heart was pounding in her throat.

"Kiss me again."

Lyle paused. He wasn't quite sure what he had heard. Or how he could cope with this challenge. Her gaze was warm and she leaned slightly towards him. He could hold on no longer. With all the power he could muster, he restrained his urgent need and controlled it. Slowly, he moved his hand around the back of her neck, pulling her closer. His eyes still locked in hers.

Their lips met in the sweetest kiss. So gentle, so tender, it made her dizzy. She opened her lips just slightly so he could deepen his kiss. His hand on her neck was the only hold she had. Her knees went weak, she wanted to sink to the floor.

Lyle pulled away first. His eyes dark. That kiss had been so insistent that he would soon have lost himself in it. In *her*.

She opened her eyes. She knew in that moment that she too wanted and would do anything with him.

"Oh." she managed with difficulty. The kiss had not been supposed to end yet, but that was all that was possible here. She had another purpose here at this party. Suddenly the rest of the evening seemed to take far too long. When she could, she sought his gaze. And he hers. They told each other from afar what they both wanted.

Finally, the last guest had left, finally they were both sitting in the taxi. There was a quaint silence. But Mel did not want to think any more that night. She felt invulnerable. She laughed to herself - what a great evening it had been. It could only get better.

Lyle looked at her from the side. She looked stunning, so happy, so free.

She met his gaze. There was no question what they were both thinking. She took his hand in hers. He held it tightly.

He gave the taxi driver the address of his hotel. The journey took what felt like hours. The way past the reception was miles long. The ride in the lift to the seventh floor seemed to take years. His door to the room didn't open for ages.

And then they were both alone in front of each other. *What now?*

"Do you want something to drink?" he suddenly asked shyly. He looked around the room as if he had forgotten where the small emergency fridge was. Unsure of what to do next. He felt like a teenager. Had spent months dreaming of having her in front of him and now he was totally unsure how to go about it.

Mel shook her head, barely noticeable.

"Hell no." were her last words before she put her arms around his neck and *kissed* him.

In that moment, all questions were answered and no doubt was left in her mind. She opened herself to him, to his passion, and gave the same. He barely suppressed a deep groan as he kissed her back. Hot fire ignited between them, he framed her face with his hands, pulling her closer. He swiftly made his way to her hair so that it fell softly and smoothly over her shoulders.

Then, inch by inch, he took on her dress, kissing and caressing, he unzipped the back of her dress and slipped it off her shoulders from her neck. He buried his face in her neck and inhaled her scent deep, deep inside him. Her smell so seductive, her skin tasted so sweet. He felt her body tremble as she responded to him and lost his control altogether.

She tugged at his tie, at his shirt, impatiently stripping both off him. It was give and take.

Lyle couldn't have enough of her, wanted to feel every single inch of her. He kissed her deeply and insistently and they soon found themselves on his bed.

Melissa was lost. Her lust matched his. Even if she had had any doubts, there was no turning back at that moment.

Her body received him willingly, her heart held him captive.

Melissa woke up. She was still in his bed, so she hadn't dreamed it up after all.

What had she *done*? Mild panic rose in her as she thought of how she had just exposed herself. Without inhibitions, without hesitation, completely and utterly. She obviously hadn't learned anything from all the heartbreak she had already gone through because of him. Was she going to be just as devastated as before? How would she ever be able to look him in the eye again after letting herself go like that?

She didn't dare move, didn't want to wake him up. Panic set in again, how would she get out of here? What would they say to each other? Was sex now part of their deal? Or was the one time actually more than enough and they had now quenched this desire for now and could go on living quietly alongside each other?

She had to get away, wanted to be alone and think about it. As carefully as she could, she got up from his bed and started to gather her things. Oh no, she would have to face the walk of shame - in yesterday's clothes, past the receptionist. She didn't have a car here, so she would have to call a taxi. She really hadn't thought this through.

"Mel?" his voice was husky. Why didn't he go back to sleep? She wasn't up to coping with his cold and distanced mood.

She froze, her things pressed in front of her chest, her hair still wild from their act filled with the most intense passion.

Lyle looked at her with a smirk. What was there to laugh about? Though laughter was better than repulsion or regret.

"Come back here." he said tantalisingly. Mel didn't budge, so he stood up and walked towards her unabashedly. Her stomach tightened. Her body was incorrigible. That one time hadn't been enough at all. It only made her desire for him worse.

"No, you won't escape me that easily. Now it's my turn." He claimed her mouth, leaving her in no doubt as to what he was about to do. She dropped her clothes and leaned against his hot, hard body.

Lyle felt her respond to him and pressed her even closer.

"You're driving me crazy." he whispered between his caresses. "I want you. Now. Tomorrow."

He gently pushed her back onto the bed, showing her how much he wanted her.

~ 122 ~

Melissa had hardly slept. They had *both* hardly slept. And it had been glorious. The thought of it still filled her with a warm, lovely feeling. A happy feeling that she didn't want to let go of.

But at some point, the next day had to begin. The bright light shone into the room and she would probably have to face Lyle's gaze. And *herself*.

She quickly ducked into the bathroom before he could stop her again. The hot rays of the shower felt good, distracted a little from her turmoil. What did *she* want? How was she going to deal with Lyle now?

In any case, she wanted to keep this nice feeling, for as long as possible.

When she re-entered the room in her bathrobe, she ground to a halt.

Before her stood Angela, in all her beauty, even now in the early hours. In front of her was Lyle, at least he had put something on. She was confused, annoyed and felt utterly exposed.

She tightened her dressing gown a little more as the other woman looked at her suspiciously. She too had not expected the younger woman to be here, it seemed.

"What is she doing here?" it escaped her.

Her tone was once again so dismissive that Mel had to grit her teeth.

"I'm sure you know what we're doing here," Lyle said jokingly.

Melissa felt the blush rise to her cheeks. Angela saw all. She was less than impressed. But also not convinced.

"So, next Saturday. You can bring *her* if you have to."

Angela turned around and walked away again. What on earth

was she doing here in his room so early? Had he known she was coming?

"What was that all about?" she asked coldly.

Lyle looked at her in amusement. He wanted nothing more than to slip the dressing gown off her shoulders and make love to her. Again. And then again.

But her look warned him that she wasn't thinking of the same thing he was.

"She was going to invite us to dinner."

"I mean, why did you let her in here when I was in the shower." She still felt like she had just stood naked in front of her enemy. "I'm not just a display."

"You always tell me I should stand by your side. I did."

"Oh no, you let her in so she could see me coming out of the shower. So she could see exactly what had been going on. You were just trying to protect your inheritance."

Melissa was disappointed and felt an immense sadness welling up inside her. Had she really expected *more*?

Lyle walked slowly towards her. She looked at him warningly.

"Do you regret it?" he asked softly. He slid his hand slowly inside her gown, placed it on her bare, hot skin. "Do you never want me to touch you again?"

His lips brushed her cheek, her neck. He opened her dressing gown fully now and caressed her tender skin.

"Do you want me to stop?"

Melissa knew he hadn't given her an answer. And the real issue was still there, but just then she couldn't think any more. Not when he touched her there, and there. She let herself be seduced on the spot.

They could talk about it later.

~ 123 ~

Melissa smiled to herself. After so many long months, today her head was not full of worries and stress about what awaited her the next day. Her heart was not heavy, full of longing for a man she could never quite have.

Today she was blissfully happy.

"Oh no, Mel!" brought Patty's friend back down to earth. It only took one look at her face and she knew exactly what had happened.

Mel let her friend enter and took refuge in the kitchen to escape the admonishing look.

"I recognise that look from here. You slept with him. Melissa McClory!"

Mel couldn't help smiling. The last two days had been so incredibly intense that she couldn't think of anything else. Even the awkward moment with Angela in his hotel room, had so quickly faded into the background as he had kissed her and caressed every part of her body. *Mel.*

"We're married." she replied weakly. She had no other excuse.

"And about to get divorced!" She was really cross with her and stood right in front of her friend, forcing her to look her in the eye. She would not drop this subject so easily. She had spent too much time with Melissa over the last few months for that and had developed a good friendship.

"Mel, don't you remember how devastated you were when you moved back here? *I* remember it very clearly. I can still see you now, all broken and torn up by grief. Because of *him.*"

Mel hadn't forgotten that either. Not a moment of it. Inside she still felt, that deep ache of loneliness, of unrequited love.

"You put all your pain and passion into your business. Look how far you've made it *without* him. Don't let him ruin it."

Mel heard every word and she agreed with her so much. Her mind was ready to give it all up again and focus fully on herself. But her heart was still trapped, was still in his hotel room, in his bed, in his arms. Where she had felt so comfortable, so *loved*.

"He said he only wanted me."

"That's called lust, Mel. Pure, animalistic lust." She had an explanation for everything and once again she was right.

"And afterwards? How was he afterwards? You're always telling me about his moods and his cold front. Did you forget about all of that because of one night?"

Mel shook her head sadly. She had wanted to push those thoughts far away, but now the doubts came back to her. Had it really only been *sex*? Or had he felt something more? Could it be that he loved her too? Or had she just seduced him and talked herself into it all because she herself was driven by animal lust?

"It felt real, this time. It was like ..."

"Like he loved you?"

"Yes! Like there really was no one else for him. Like he only sees me and wants me." Mel felt this deep tug in her heart. Wanted so badly to believe what had happened was real.

"And not Verona?"

That had hit home. Mel backed away a little at that question. This woman, this thorn in their relationship, she had repressed altogether, not daring to question it again too closely.

"Patty..." she pleaded softly. She felt cornered.

"Of course, he said exactly what you wanted to hear. And maybe in that moment he truly meant it. Who wouldn't when you're so close to getting what you lust after! But in the end, *he* decides where and when. Try it the other way round! Then you'll see how quickly he rejects you."

Mel rubbed her eyes wearily. Had he decided where and when? After all, it was she who had asked him to kiss her. But only after he had come back into her life, only after he knew she had not had an affair with Roger and only after he had promised to seduce her. Had he planned all this?

"I didn't resist for a second," she said softly. Not the first time, or the other times thereafter.

"I don't want to have to scrape you up off the curb again. I want you to be aware of what it means, every step of the way. You know he let you go. What can that possibly mean for your future?"

"I know what I'm doing. And what I won't." she replied strongly. She looked deep into her friend's eyes. "I know what will come out of it in the end. I am fully aware of that. But for now, *he is here*. He followed me, albeit after six months and fifteen days." She smirked at the memory, at his words. "He wants me by his side while he's here, and so do I."

For Mel, that was the end of the subject. Her friend saw it in her eyes.

Patty put her hand on her shoulders amicably.

"Was it ecstatic?" Her eyes sparkled.

"Like never before."

They both laughed the dull thoughts away.

~ 124 ~

Melissa could not believe her ears. A television programme wanted to film her business and broadcast it to the world during the news. The long weeks of endless hours at work paid off.

She literally laughed as she talked to this nice man from the filming company. It would only be ten short minutes on TV, but it was going to be a whole day here in their building. They were going to film some clips of the different classes, the rooms, the pictures and the stories, as well as the teachers and of course, the company's head, Melissa McClory.

She was so excited, she had to stand up. She hadn't expected it at all, not yet. At some point, it had been on her schedule to advertise on television as well, but that had not been scheduled until winter or spring.

Melissa checked her calendar to see when it would be most convenient.

"And while you're at it, can you confirm the date when we can hold the interview with your husband?"

Her joy vanished in an instant. *Lyle.*

That selfish, sneaky type of a man. Had he arranged all this behind her back while they had been at her party? Had he only brought up this possibility again for himself to advertise himself? Had he not kept to the rules after all?

She was furious and wanted to cancel the whole thing immediately. However, she had to remind herself once again what was good for her company and what was her personal problem.

"Lyle also thinks I'm his private secretary, but that's not entirely true. You'll have to call on her. I'm afraid I don't know his schedule by heart."

The man on the other end laughed, seeming to have taken it as a joke. That was how she had meant it.

They agreed on a convenient time for everyone and Mel hung up with satisfaction.

You wait, I won't let you get away with that.

<h1 style="text-align:center">~ 125 ~</h1>

He came as expected. Her call to his secretary to say she couldn't go to dinner this week had worked.

Melissa was still working on the next displays with Joshua. She had purposely not let him go home until Lyle got there. She was tired of always being the one who had to sacrifice something.

The look on his face told her everything. He had little patience when he was in a good mood, but right now he looked totally as if he was about to lose his shit.

She smiled at Joshua and suggested he go home. He gladly accepted the suggestion, although he would have liked to see how the two of them would get on today. The tension could literally be felt in the air. One spark and it would be over. That's what he called a passionate marriage.

Lyle waited for him to be gone. He narrowed his eyes. He didn't even know what to be angry with first.

"Just you and him alone again?"

"Still him. And jealous again?"

He shook his head.

"We've been over that."

"Apparently not, since you've started it again."

She set about putting the pictures away neatly, only to have him wait some more. She heard him take a deep breath in and out. She wore her hair in a ponytail, her neck exposed and seductive in front of him. She had some paint on her arm and hands. He needed to distract himself.

"I got your message." He finally said to get to the point. She was at the other end of the room, yet not far enough away that he couldn't smell her. "Can you explain to me why you shouldn't be available this weekend? As my wife?"

Mel felt a hot tingle run through her. The thought of spending the weekend with him, and as his wife, was tempting. Too tempting. She had to force herself to find her anger and resentment again. That was why she had lured him here.

She propped her hands on her hips and looked at him with an ice-cold stare. This was not at all how he had imagined their next get-together. He had gone through completely different fantasies of how he could possibly have her all to himself again. That was clearly not the case today.

"Did you stick to the rules then?"

He looked at her puzzled for a moment, not quite sure what she was talking about.

"You know, as well as I do, that we were both quite willing."

A blush leapt to her face. Her stomach tightened lustfully.

"*That's* not what I'm talking about." She swallowed and once again had to push the memories far away to focus on their argument. "You promised you wouldn't interfere with my business. And what do I hear today? You promised all kinds of people an interview as long as they are sweet to me!"

Now he remembered one or two people where he had probably advertised a little too much. He had considered that perfectly innocent. A small thing. It hadn't stuck in his mind at all. The night and day with her, on the other hand....

"There's no harm in it."

"But that's not what I wanted," she retorted sharply. "This is Melissa's Easy Art Easy Heart - not the McClory Foundation. Remember that?"

"There is no difference in it. We both stand for what's best for children. The stories I sell go to charity just the same."

She would have liked to shake him if she hadn't been trying hard not to step within his reach.

"But you don't just write stories. You're an international bestseller of novels. Everyone wants a bit of your fame and they come here now because of *you*. And don't see what *I'm* doing here for the children."

"But I can mention it in my interviews."

"No!" she almost shouted. She was actually truly angry now and was close to throwing the paint brushes at his expensive suit. "I don't want you to associate with me at all. This company is completely independent of you, so if-"

"If what?" he interrupted suddenly. His eyes sparkled with suppressed anger. He had only been waiting for her to show her true cards again. "In case we get divorced? That's what this is all about, isn't it? You want to keep your business separate from me so you can disappear just like that and everything will go on as normal for you."

Mel stared at him in shock. There was some truth to it, but it sounded so calculating the way he put it. Was that it? Was that her intention?

No, she wanted to be able to keep something of value when he dumped her and she would be devastated. Then at least she wanted to still have something that belonged to her. Because all her pride, strength and reason for living would then no longer exist. Her art would then be the last thing she had left.

Deeply stressed, Lyle ran a hand through his hair. Then he looked at her again with an unreadable impression on his face.

"Even after *that* night, you can't imagine a life by my side? We have money, fame, both of us, we have passion. That was the deal. Surely such a pretend marriage couldn't go any better. I can give you everything."

Mel's heart was breaking. Except what I want. Your *love*.

"So you decide my whole life. What I do, when and with whom?"

"Only with me."

She hesitated at his answer.

"And if you fall in love, or I ... myself?"

"That's out of the question. For both of us."

Mel had known all this, yet had chosen to ignore it. Hearing it again made it not only worse, but true.

"I need time."

"You have until Friday night."

"And if I don't come?"

Lyle didn't know the answer to that either. It caused him great panic, the thought of her not coming. How could he make sure she stayed by his side?

"Think of your children. And what you could offer them on your own."

Mel looked after him, bitterly appalled. That hadn't been fair. He was in complete control of her. Maybe she had to try her friend's theory after all. Once she decided who wanted something with whom and when, would he be able to resist her or would she have him in the palm of her hand?

~ 126 ~

Melissa deliberately chose a short, simple dress. It needed no embellishments, needed no jewellery. It showed as much leg as she had ever considered wearing. She refrained from wearing tights, sticking to the minimal outfit. Either way, she would not be able to keep up with others in this silver dress. Why overdo it?

She tried something new with her hair, choosing a side-tail that rested loosely on her shoulder. But after a long look in the mirror, she felt too dolled up, and put her hair back in a bun. That was the way she felt most comfortable.

The taxi arrived on time to pick her up, but to her disappointment, Lyle wasn't in it. He would probably meet her at the dinner party, she thought hopefully and nervously. That meant she would have to enter the grand hall alone. Everyone would be staring at her, at how she arrived and what she was wearing. Had the short length of her dress been too daring after all? Was it too late to change again?

She was glad it was outside her normal area this time. The drive was long enough that she was sure she wouldn't meet anyone there who knew her or could somehow connect her with her company. That was just as well. She embarrassed herself all the time at these kinds of events and wouldn't be able to take it if she gave the wrong impression, in front of her future clients or co-workers.

After an hour's drive, her nerves returned. She hesitated for a moment before feeling confident enough to get out. She saw the huge theatre in front of her and several people were milling around in front of it. All had at least one person on their arms.

No one seemed alone. Just *her*.

Get a grip, she told herself. She would find him soon enough, there won't be that many people here.

She couldn't have been more wrong. The whole auditorium, the enormous hall was teeming with people. Famous writers and journalists, various editors and managers, small entrepreneurs who wanted to pick up a new author effortlessly and cheaply. And their life companions, obediently went unheard alongside, smartly dressed from top to bottom, some with eager facial expressions if they were desperate for a new contract and some with long faces, of those who regularly attend such events but didn't really need it anymore because they already had more than enough money and fame.

And now she was there too. No sign of Lyle. She saw Angela and Kurt from afar, but she took the longest route to avoid them at all costs.

She grabbed a glass of orange juice from a tray and pondered how best to proceed. Finally, courage seized her and she joined the couple with the most bored faces and talked to them about Melissa's Easy Art Easy Heart. This kind of collaboration seemed to appeal to some, and her company was well received. Some offered to write stories or comic strips to go with her paintings. They promised to get back to her. Mel laughed delightedly. Maybe this evening wasn't so bad for her.

"You did come." Lyle whispered in her ear. He had approached her unnoticed. She didn't see him, but smelled his aftershave the second he was behind her.

Instantly she got goosebumps and her body was willing. She had completely forgotten to keep looking for him after her first few conversations had gone so well. Bad wife.

She didn't move, looking at the other people who seemed to be having a good time.

"You made it perfectly clear that I'm nothing without you, didn't you?" she countered softly, but her cold words were clear enough to hear.

She could feel him right behind her. His hot body was millimetres away from her. All she had to do was lean back a little and she would be lost.

She took a step forward. Just as Angela and Kurt saw her. Lyle put his arm around her waist possessively. She hated this show, but didn't resist.

"Not in a bathrobe today." She looked down at her dismissively. Clearly, she was not at all impressed with her dress and appearance. Unlike her, Angela looked stunningly beautiful. She was wearing a tight, strapless dress. Her bare shoulders must have had fairy glitter on them because they sparkled in the light. Yes, it would certainly never occur to her to do something like *that*.

"Not until later," Mel countered. Lyle stiffened noticeably beside her.

Angela had understood the meaning all too well, and Kurt smirked to himself. She liked him. He was normal.

"Lyle, don't forget you still have to talk to Jonathan Blake. He's the most important guest tonight. He's been turning the kids' events into a TV gig for the last couple of years. You should be part of it."

Kurt briefly told her about the achievements of this Mr Blake, as Melissa herself had not heard much about it. This event seemed like a good idea in principle. But Mel doubted how much this public attention was really for the children, or rather for the man himself. She looked Lyle in the eye to ask him, but he only had eyes for Angela.

They were talking about something, which made her laugh. It was so *fake* and on top of that she placed one of her freshly manicured hands on *his* shoulder and she leaned towards him. Yes, it was clear how she was flirting with him. Kurt turned away a little, he too had seen it and was embarrassed.

"Luckily *he* only has eyes for *you*," he said quietly. Melissa wasn't so sure.

At that moment their eyes met. For a moment, time seemed to stand still and she could have sworn that his look said more than he always wanted to admit. She smiled ever so slightly to tell him, yes, I am here.

The moment was over just as quickly as it had started and the meal began. They all sat together at round tables, yet so far apart. The menu was not bad at all. There were several courses, fortunately, so she hoped that even after the salad and some fish, she might still be full. She amused herself by talking about her project, in which Kurt seemed really interested. He even had one or two suggestions she wanted to try and incorporate. And he also knew a couple of cartoon artists who might be able to teach a class or two. She was very grateful to him.

Lyle had been watching her the whole time, even when Angela had done her best to chat him up all evening, he hadn't taken his eyes off her for a second. She looked so gorgeous. He regretted that they had to sit so far apart, at events like this. He couldn't stroke her legs under the table. Wanted so much to feel her bare skin under her dress. The short length had not escaped him at all. It had not escaped *anyone*; he was sure of that. But she was his. His gaze rested on her face as she looked up. Her smile persisted and she bit her lips mischievously. Before Angela distracted him again and he had to down his glass to get back some sort of self-control.

Melissa turned her attention back to Kurt, who was not blind. He felt the attraction between them and envied it.

The evening went on and on. Lyle left after dinner to do more rounds. He still had to see the most important man of the evening. He did so reluctantly, for his mind was no longer quite on the matter.

Melissa excused herself from the two and continued to try her luck with a few journalists. They had perked up when she mentioned her name, less so when she spoke of her company.

"So you are his wife. How long have you been married? Do you live permanently here in Frankenberg now?"

Melissa only barely answered the questions. Two years or so, and for the moment, yes. She was not prepared for this kind of conversation. She did her best to tell them more of her interest, but soon realised it was pointless.

Out of the corner of her eye, she saw Lyle. Her husband. And all at once she knew exactly what she wanted. She wanted this show to become real, too.

What did Patty say? You should decide when and where. Let's see if he did go along.

Melissa had had enough of this evening. She assumed that Lyle had finally found that important guy and that was why he had been talking to him for so long. All right, he had had his chance to introduce himself, now it was her turn.

Heart pounding, she walked towards the circle and stood right next to her husband. Lyle looked at her a little surprised, maybe even a little annoyed, but she was unfazed.

"This is Melissa -"

"I'm his wife." she interrupted him confidently, smiling at the older man. He had silver-grey hair, wore tailored clothes and his hand was so soft it made her uncomfortable holding it.

"How ... amazing to meet you." He said charmingly. Her dress had not gone unnoticed. She wanted to tug at it herself but pulled herself together.

The conversation continued and more and more she got the impression that this was about money. Not for the children, not for their needs, but his.

Melissa took courage.

She stood on her tiptoes to whisper just one word in Lyle's ear. "Unbearable."

She then apologised to everyone and walked away with her head held high. Inside she was a wreck, a total nervous wreck and deeply aroused. No idea if he would understand her hidden message. Maybe all this was so long in the past ...

She chose the nearest exit and stood at the end of the corridor. The evening was still in full swing, so the hallway was positively empty. One person came by to go to the toilet. Otherwise, she was alone.

She began to doubt her idea. Regretted her directness and audacity.

Then he was standing in front of her. *Lyle.*

His gaze dark, his body strong and powerful. Just as she wanted him. He saw her face, could read her mind.

"Oh no, you won't change your mind on me now."

In one step he was with her, pulling her into his arms. His kiss was so insistent that all her doubts evaporated and deepest passion replaced them. He momentarily stopped the kiss to catch his breath, saw a door to the adjacent cleaning room and pulled her in with him.

Melissa watched him lock the door. It didn't take her a second and she was coming towards him when he turned back to her.

She ran her hands wildly through his hair, making him lose his mind. His hands were everywhere, finally on her leg, her bare leg, and he let his fingers slide teasingly along her skin, all the way under her dress. She sighed softly as he touched her where her fire burned. He pressed her against the wall, his kisses becoming deeper and more explicit. She brought him the same passion. Drove him mad.

Lyle had just enough strength to leave her for a moment and look into her eyes. She opened them languidly, completely out of breath. Her whole body wanted him.

"Mel?"

"Take me." she said unequivocally and Lyle didn't hesitate another moment. He brought his lips down hard on hers to try and keep as quiet as possible. She was so infatuating, so excitingly beautiful, that he simply lost himself in her.

He held her in his arms for a long time afterwards, trying to steady his breathing again.

Their bodies were still vibrating.

Silently they smoothed out their clothes. Her hair. She didn't dare look at him. She wasn't quite sure what had gotten into her. In any case, they had both lost control. It had been mutual.

She took a deep breath, and exhaled slowly. She had no idea what she looked like now. It was quite dark in this storage room here. And untidy. She hadn't noticed that before.

Lyle opened the door and stepped out first. Given that the hallway was clear, she followed him. Back in the light, she was very aware of what he could probably see now.

He stopped her when she tried to leave in a hurry. Anywhere but here alone with him. She needed a moment to forgive herself. But he did not let her go.

He stood before her, so amazingly strong, again just what she needed. He lifted her chin with his fingers and smiled. His eyes were dark, unreadable.

Her cheeks were flushed and she looked a thousand times more adorable with the little strands that had escaped from her bun.

"This guest is really important. Next time-" he said softly and Mel held her breath. It almost sounded like a warning. She wasn't sure he would approve of a next time. She had, after all, taken him away from his important guest. "... we have to be a little patient, and find a more comfortable place. Then we can really savour and enjoy it."

He gave her another kiss that told her his hunger for her was far from satisfied.

He eased away from her but she did the same and stopped *him* this time.

"Stay." She kissed him passionately. He forgot everything around him. There was only her and her scent, her body, her warmth. He obeyed only too willingly. His hands framed her face. They were both on fire again.

"Lyle. Jonathan wants to say goodbye."

They both stepped away from each other as if they had been burned. They had totally forgotten where they were. Angela stared at them coldly. It hadn't pleased her at all to find the two of them so close. Not at all. What was it about this plain brat that he couldn't resist? What on earth did he see in her? Surely it was just sex. He could find that anywhere. With *any* woman.

Lyle looked deep into Melissa's eyes once more, as if apologising to her. She took a step back to get out of his way.

Lyle straightened his suit once more and left. Angela stayed, her gaze full of disgust and hatred.

"Yeah, he's good at that, isn't he? Don't flatter yourself. You're not the first to lose your head when it comes to Lyle. And I guarantee you, you won't be the last."

With those cutting words, she left her rival standing.
Melissa fled to the bathroom to calm her nerves and body. She looked at her reflection in shock. Was it really all *not* real? Was it really just lust driving him, driving them both? Were they just passing the time? No, it couldn't be, she was *wearing* his ring. Continuously, he was making sure that this marriage had to look real. Surely that also meant he couldn't play games with others.
She felt sick at the thought of him behaving like that with another woman. She couldn't bear that idea.

~ 127 ~

The work was fulfilling: her children were unique and cheerful, the reports about her business in the newspapers were praising and her successes were regular. And her marriage was...

Mel felt the heat rise to her face and her stomach tighten at the memory of what had happened in the storeroom. It had been a few days since their last evening together. Surely it had to be time to see him again soon. Was she ready for that? Especially after Angela's cold statement, would she approach him about it or continue to ignore it? Would he want to follow up on what they had started on Saturday? Did she have the will, the self-control to avoid him?

She just didn't know what was best anymore. How could a man show so much desire for her and *not* love her? Surely that was not possible. Should she approach him about *that*? Had she forgotten that he had made it quite clear that there would never be anything more between them? But maybe she could manage to win him over after all. Next time she wouldn't give in completely, and maybe ask for dinner alone.

She didn't have to worry about what she did or didn't ask him. He didn't come over that week, didn't call either.

The weekend passed and the next week began. The days grew longer, the nights shorter. Fortunately. She had far too much time at night to think of him, to *miss* him. She needed to distract herself more. Patty had probably been right after all. He decided what happened when, he handled her life how and when he wanted. That had to end.

Yes, she had more than enjoyed the sex with him, but that was over now. She couldn't let herself be seduced or seduce him *again*. Not if that meant he would leave her for weeks without contacting her. She didn't have the strength for *that*. She would not put up with *that*.

They had both tasted each other one more time, now they had to stick to the strict agreements again. It hadn't been that *special*, had it?

Angela's cold but perhaps true words rang in her ears. She knew she wasn't the first, but had always been able to convince herself that he wouldn't betray her after all. Now she was no longer so sure. No news for a fortnight. Why didn't he come running? Didn't he think about her as often as she thought about him?

Melissa slammed the cupboard door a little louder than she had intended. She'd spent enough energy on being annoyed, not focussed, now it was her children's turn again.

She spent the rest of the day with her class. Some of these kids had been coming since she opened a few months ago. It filled her with pride that they still looked as happy as they had in the beginning. Except for one little boy who kept cowering in the corner and not talking to the others. This class had children between five and six years old. But he was a little smaller than the others, much quieter and always alone. She had watched him from afar before, but today she was a little more worried than usual. His clothes still had the same paint stains from last week, and his skin also seemed unclean and his hair unkempt.

Melissa suspected the worst. She took her chance to talk to him as the others began their still life. He was so quiet that she squatted down next to him to hear him. He described his painting, in great detail. He had thought carefully about how he would present it and chose his colours carefully to do so. But his brushstrokes were coarse and he could not reproduce what he had imagined. Out of anger or frustration, he knocked over his canvas and gave it one *good* kick.

Melissa was startled for a moment at how this quiet little boy could muster such reactions and then she smiled encouragingly at him. She picked up the canvas again and placed his picture on it. She invited him to continue telling his story and as she listened, she painted what he described.

When his father finally came to fetch him, she took him aside for a moment. He was not at all impressed by this, his dismissive expression not hiding how much he disliked it.

"Mr Mueller." she said kindly, flashing a nice smile. "I just have to say how impressed I am with your son. Look at the imagination in his painting."

The father seemed impatient and uninterested. Just nodded towards him indicating that he should long be done washing his hands after all and he should be ready to leave.

"That's not his picture. He can't draw things like that."

"They were his ideas, I helped him put them on paper." She confirmed and took a deep breath. "Seb was a little disappointed that he couldn't paint it himself and showed a somewhat ... aggressive reaction today."

The man in front of her, who couldn't have been much older than the early twenties, glanced at her briefly from the side, as if she'd caught him doing something.

"So?"

"Seb deliberately knocked over his canvas and took his *anger* out on it. Maybe you could talk to him about it, and explain that there are other ways to deal with his frustration."

He stared at her angrily. He wasn't even thinking about it.

"Fine. He's not coming back."

He grabbed his boy by the arm and pulled him away, Melissa running after him. She hadn't meant it that way. The last thing she wanted was to *not* see Seb again and have his father punish him for it.

"Of course, he's still welcome here. I can personally help him turn his stories onto paper."

Seb looked up at her and was only too happy to agree. But his father had heard enough.

"That's only too generous of you. And then, behind our back, you call Social Services about aggressive behaviour. No, thanks. We won't be back."

With that, he had stepped into the lift and the doors closed in front of her.

Melissa resisted the temptation to press the button and come after them again. But she *had* to leave it at that. *Had to*. She had caused enough damage. Today she had failed her children.

The gloomy mood hung onto her until after work. Ally and Josh were kind enough to help her clean up, but her heavy thoughts were still with Seb. He deserved more. Why hadn't she thought about what she said to the father and *how* she should approach that matter? Couldn't she have guessed that he would react like that because he felt attacked himself? Of course, he would immediately leave so as not to draw attention to himself and his child.

She felt terribly guilty.

"Oh hello, Mr McClory. How nice to see you!" Ally exclaimed delightedly. Her cheeks glowed red and she beamed her best smile. She took the chance to talk to him for a moment, telling him about the successful day they had.

Mel looked up briefly and then away again. That was all she needed.

Lyle listened patiently to the young woman, even giving her a smile before finally joining his wife. All under the strictest scrutiny of Ally, who had lost her own smile. Melissa did not seem happy to see him *at all*. What a way to behave!

"Mel?" he greeted softly and gave her little kiss on the cheek. Mel mustered all her strength not to turn her head. She was only more than aware of the looks on her staff's faces. His aftershave already filled the air. Don't get involved with him again!

"We still have work to do." she said kindly but curtly. Lyle sensed her distance instantly. He had waited too long to seek her out after all. He had longed for her *every day*, didn't want to be separated from her for a second, but it couldn't go on like this. They needed some distance, otherwise they might lose that …. spark and not appear so good in front of others. That was the *only* reason he had stayed away. For *no* other reason.

He took off his jacket and loosened his tie. All this did not go unnoticed, especially by Ally who kept giving him a few glances.

Josh remained silent and sorted through the pictures. Lyle set about looking at the best-chosen ones and just for the sake of it wrote a few stories about them and put them on a piece of paper to go with them. He was *amazing*. Mel!

Soon everyone had finished and only Mel and Lyle remained. One too many, she thought angrily. Why had he stayed? Why did he have to loosen his tie, didn't he know it made him look even more attractive? His hair lay wildly on his head, he looked tired. He glanced at her.

"Are you all right, Mel?" he asked when he saw her pucker. She seemed a little calmer than usual. Something seemed to be on her mind. His absence? How could he explain that he wanted her more every day but *couldn't* let it happen?

"You had to show up today, of course." came her cold reply. "Not before, and not after."

Yes, she was angry with him. Rightly so.

"I wanted to see you."

"Only now? After almost two weeks? How have you been enjoying yourself in that time? Or with whom?"

"Our arrangement is based on business evenings and events," he reminded her.

"That's right. Nothing more."

"Unless we both want to."

"No, no more. I'm not waiting here for you until you lust after me again."

"Fine."

This was not how their reunion was supposed to turn out, quite the opposite. He had had very different ideas, all absolutely immensely satisfying. He looked at her sombrely and saw past her anger.

"So what else is going on?"

Melissa was surprised. Could he really sense that her head was somewhere else? That she was still thinking about Seb and *her* failure? If he could show such a sensitive side to him, why could he turn his back on her for so long?

"A little boy. He... I..." She shook her head. How was she supposed to express all she'd screwed up today?

Lyle looked at her encouragingly. Gone was the cold gaze and the anger. He seemed to really want to know what was weighing on her mind.

"What's his name? What happened?"

"Seb and I let him down." she answered first and then explained to him in a condensed version what had happened, still disappointed with herself and just *bitter*. "He needs help, support … *love*. I could have given him that, here, every week. Little by little I could have gained his trust, and maybe I could have healed his world. I could have been there for him."

"Mel, you were there for him. Are here for all these children. Your classes are for all of them, whether they have money or not. You're already offering them all of that."

She didn't quite hear him. She was sad and tired.

"He needs better surroundings. I-"

"You can't offer all children a new home, you can't want to adopt every child just because they're unwashed and unkempt."

"He's so helpless."

Lyle hesitated for a moment, ran his fingers nervously through his hair, then looked at her frankly.

"We haven't talked about that side of the contract yet, but if you want or feel the urge… I mean, we can discuss children too." He sounded all embarrassed, and looked even more awkward. "What I'm saying is …. we can have children too…. Soon or whenever….."

She stared at him with wide eyes. He could not be serious. He was going to *discuss* whether they would have children? There had never been any talk of that. Had he lost his bloody mind?

"We can *discuss* the matter?" she asked incredulously.

"Of course, then we would have to extend our agreement once again. Several times probably, for months. Who knows."

"Stop." she interrupted his confused ramblings. "I don't *want* to bring children into the world."

Her icy tone and stark determination struck him right into his core. He was no longer awkward. Was acutely aware of her answer.

"You mean, not with me." came his equally cold remark.

Melissa held his dismissive gaze. Her expression was unmoved. She showed no doubt or any sign that she might change her mind.

"You and me, that's the last thing we need in our show marriage. Involving innocent children." She admitted. "No, not with you." She grabbed her handbag and her jacket, with this final decision she left him standing there. It was settled for her. There had never been any question of her wanting to have children. Especially not in a marriage that meant nothing and existed only for financial gain. She had not considered children for years. She had learned her lesson agonisingly.

~ 128 ~

Melissa stood angrily in front of the mirror. She was dressed in a short, summery dress. Had done her hair and put on some mascara. And why? *For him!* For her dear husband, who had not even thought it necessary to ask her personally if she could come with him to an important event this weekend. Oh no, his attractive secretary had informed her. When, where and for how long. Admittedly, she had used the phone call to have a really good chat with Joyce Miller and catch up on everything that had been going on lately. She missed the woman and their gossip and coffee afternoons. But that did*n't* matter. He should have asked her himself.

At least this time it wasn't a boring, stiff dinner, but an afternoon in some suburb where they were supposed to do all kinds of activities so that lots and lots of donations could be collected. Especially if there was a successful children's author involved and committed to helping children in need. Right up her street. Damn, he had her! And he *knew* it.

And now she was standing there like a puppet. Waiting for the taxi, waiting for further instructions. She just let herself be ordered around, and it bothered her so much that she almost ignored the bell. She wanted to show him, that he couldn't just expect her to jump when he called. She had her own plans. And on top of that, the last meeting lay still heavy in her stomach. How had they gone from a deeply arousing moment in the storeroom to this freezing cold conversation, yet again? Why couldn't they get along well for two consecutive days? What was *still* keeping them apart?

Mel hesitated a moment longer as the doorbell shrilled a second time. She had no other choice, she told herself desperately. She could not and would not jeopardise her business. It was still far too young for her to find sponsors in any other way. Perhaps in time, with her reputation and success, that would be a possibility. But not yet today.

Lyle had stepped out of the taxi to help her into the car personally. The expression on his face was neutral when she finally appeared. And then it showed some relief, and something else she couldn't interpret, when he saw her in her simple but colourful dress. She had put her hair in a side braid. Her neck was so rapturously exposed. He was strongly tempted to bury his face in her neck and taste her skin. Her gaze, however, was so cold and dismissing that he did not respond to his desire and instead just nodded at her.

This could be a *long* day, he thought to himself as they got into the taxi without a word.

"The local papers will be there," he finally said when he could no longer stand the silence.

"I know what you expect of me," she countered tersely, so that he didn't have to say anything else.

The ride seemed never-ending. They finally arrived at the big field where the tents and stations were all set up already, a lot of people seemed to be having a great time already. A couple of small carousels were there too, face painting, balloon modelling and lots of little reading stations. A DJ was even playing some music on a small stage and quite a few children and adults were already dancing happily to it. Somewhere at the edge of the field they had also set up a makeshift car wash where you could get your car cleaned up a bit.

It looked rousingly cheerful. She had to admit that. She was glad she had opted for her loose summer dress. The sun was beating down from the sky and it was definitely not the weather for an uncomfortable evening dress.

Lyle hesitated for a moment as they both got out of the car and it started to drive off. He was aware that she would much rather be somewhere else, but he wanted her here by his side.

Mel felt his presence intensely, could smell him. He looked even better today, in his shorts and a T-shirt. She couldn't remember the last time she had seen him so casual. Maybe never! Well, he was just doing everything to fit in with this show here. It was all for the others, nothing was real.

Mel got it over with and grabbed his hand. She ignored the overwhelming tingling in her stomach as she felt his hand in hers, fingers interlocking. She had to get through this today.

"Come on then, let's join in."

Lyle resisted the urge to pull her close and kiss her. He had her hand for now and her right next to him. He had to be *content* with that.

Melissa had to admit to herself that she had a great afternoon. She thought all the different stations were really well organised. The people were all friendly and encouraging, and most importantly, they all really did it for the children. Every activity was offered for free and the smiles on their faces were the payment. She let herself be persuaded to have something painted on her face too. The little butterfly on her cheek looked good on her. Then Melissa had also given free rein to her art and painted up two or three pictures as an idea. It was great fun and also a way to talk about her company. They all heard *her* name, not just McClory.

As she said goodbye to them again and was about to make her way to the next tent, Lyle held her back. Her smile was still on her face, her joy genuine. His gaze was dark, never taking his eyes off her. She felt her stomach tighten.

Damn it, how *could* her body betray her like this? Did it have to respond to him so willingly? When would she finally learn?

He grabbed her hand again and pulled her closer. He felt her slight resistance, didn't like it *at all*. But she didn't resist very hard and their bodies were now only a few millimetres apart.

"Here I can touch you without you running away from me," he whispered hotly in her ear. His breath so hot that it gave her goosebumps even in that heat.

Mel would have liked to sink to the floor, her knees so soft. Her body so weak.

He gave her a light kiss on the cheek. So light and yet so sweet that it took her breath away. Then, without further arousing touches, they walked to the next station together. Mel's head was spinning, she swore he would *regret* this. What he could do to her, she could do just as well.

They showed their faces everywhere, together as a loving couple, holding hands and never apart. Every now and then he stole a little kiss or touched her hip, or her back. He knew exactly what he was doing to her. She was on fire. She just needed a moment where she could steal his senses as much as he was stealing hers. Let's see how he would like that.

A short while later it was his moment to read out one of his new stories. The children and adults listened to him with rapt attention. Mel was all in too, and would have fallen in love with him all over again if she hadn't already been hopelessly there. His manner in front of these children was infectious and honest. Like a completely different person. *Lyle*....

The organisers praised his stories and advertised even more.

"And also a big thank you to Mr McClory for making this children's festival possible for us today. The event was personally funded by him and *all* donations will go on to our children. Thank you, Lyle."

This particular voice had been stuck in her head for a while now. She saw a middle-age woman on stage, the woman in charge of this event and the other voice during her phone call with Lyle. One look and she realised her utter error and embarrassment.

Mel looked at him in shock. She automatically applauded along as she realised that he had organised and funded all this. Was that why he hadn't had time for his wife? Was that why he was untraceable every day? Had her anger been *unjustified*?

No, a phone call doesn't take long. Neither does a kiss. He should have made an effort, especially after their hot encounter. She forgave him nothing.

It took Lyle several minutes before he could seek her out again. The many visitors still wanted to thank him, congratulate him or just say hello. He smiled throughout, was friendly and took his time with everyone. He had a great way with the children.

Her anger was wavering again. Finally, he was by her side again. His eyes were shining.

Before she could say anything, they were approached by the local photographer and asked to stand together for a photo.

Lyle immediately pulled her close, a little too close, she thought.

"Smile, my wife." he whispered in her ear.

She did as he told her, although at that moment it wasn't that hard. She stepped away from him again as soon as the photographer was satisfied with his picture.

"Did you want to leave already?" he asked cautiously. He hoped she wanted to stay. He enjoyed her next to him, near him, simply knowing she was there. He was far from tired of her.

Mel shook her head. She nodded in the direction of the car wash. The sun was burning so hot from the sky that she would find it pleasant to wash a few cars.

"Let's do that next!" she suggested, taking his hand and pulling him along. He laughed to himself. He would have done anything she suggested at that moment.

As they got closer, they first saw what a filthy state these vehicles were in and that it would probably be more than a few minutes. On top of that, they were provided with buckets of water, no hose. The foam was bubbling over and they had the smallest of cloths in their hands. Mel laughed when she saw the look on Lyle's face after he wrung out the rag and barely anything was left. They chose one of the smaller cars and gave it their best shot. But the foam could not be wiped away, the dirt even less. After several attempts, there was more soap in their hair than in the bucket. Mel was still laughing and Lyle shook his head playfully. He splashed some water in her direction to stop her from laughing, but that only made it more amusing. He took the bucket and emptied it over the protective bonnet. It was all to no avail.

Mel walked up to him and took the rag from his hand. His hair was wet, he had dirt on his cheek and she didn't look much better.

"You can't escape me here either." she said firmly and kissed him before he could recover from his shock.

It only took a second before she felt his arms around her and he was swept away by her kiss. His hands moved to her back, to her hip and pressed her close. There was no doubt that he felt the same as she did. Within seconds, the desire for each other was so great that for a moment they forgot where they were.

Mel braced her hands against his chest and gently pushed him off her. Her breath hitched; her heart pounded. She didn't know what he could read in her eyes now, so she looked down to the ground.

She was torn. She wanted to feel him, no question about it, wanted more than just a kiss. But most of all she wanted him, the man who laughed with others and could be free. The man who had time for everyone, and stood up for them. She didn't want this spectacle. That was not enough.

"This was a mistake." she said plainly.

Lyle had hoped to hear anything but that. He sobered instantly, hiding his disappointment behind his cold reproach.

"Yours. Not mine."

Mel took a step away from him, aware that all the people were watching them. That they had seen it all and *would* see it all. It cost her everything to not just turn and run. Instead, she lifted her chin and smiled at him, but her eyes remained sad.

"Is the game over for today?" she asked quietly, so that no one could see what she was saying and yet would assume that they were just confessing their love. Meanwhile, they grew more and more distant from each other.

They lasted another half hour together. Side by side, hands joined, but then it was over. Until the next time.

~ 129 ~

Summer was in full swing. With summer came the summer holidays and new classes and adventures to experience. Melissa threw herself headlong into her work, every day and every night. She had no time to think about her marriage, or the absence of Lyle. It was the same as before. A ring on her hand, but no man to go with it. It was much better that way, much more bearable than his proximity. She knew very well that she would never be able to resist him for any substantial amount of time. Fortunately, she didn't have to worry about that, he was never *there*. Once in a while she had to accompany him to a dinner. Here and there a call from his secretary but that was it. Melissa had no problems with it, hardly missed him. Just a little.

Actually, totally .... utterly ... constantly.

But she still had enough pride and dignity left in her that she wouldn't make the first move and beg for a rendezvous. No, there was no bloody way. He would turn up again at some point. At the latest when people started talking about their distant marriage. As her employees surely did. They saw first and foremost how much time she spent at work and how much of it *alone*.

Today she had to push those rotten thoughts away. It was a new class, a new trial - getting parents and children on board. The same principle, but everyone working together. She had gathered several ideas together as starter activities, and each family could choose their own materials to work with. It was an all-day class at the weekend, so all parents or guardians had a chance to join in too. Which, of course, might mean she'd have to cancel on Lyle if he happens to be needing her on a Saturday.

Tough luck for him, she told herself defiantly. Her families came first.

Melissa had a good feeling about this event. Had been preparing for it for days and had invested hours in making sure everything would go smoothly. Her best employees had volunteered to help out, paid of course. But that didn't matter. She would worry about wages another time. Her financial side of the business was a bit of a sore point. She would probably have to take Lyle's money after all. She would worry about that next time. Today had to go by successfully first.

She was checking the equipment again when Lyle appeared. As if she had sensed it. She shot him a warning look.

For weeks he doesn't show his face, and then he shows up here and what? Her heart was instantly back at his feet and she wanted to run, like a princess, into his arms and confess her undying love. *Damn it.*

Lyle looked at the hall and her preparations. He was a little confused to find her here working. That would explain why he hadn't been able to reach her at her flat.

"What's going on? It's Saturday."

Melissa couldn't help but smile proudly when she told him about her new class. She was full of excitement all at once and struggled not to grin.

"And that will last for how long?"

Mel didn't let herself be fazed. This was her plan and her job. No matter what he wanted her to do. It was obvious that he was only here expecting her services, otherwise he never showed his face voluntarily.

"All day. There will be refreshments and even a packed lunch. It's going to be great."

Lyle was almost infected by her cheerfulness.

"Can I help?"

She stared at his face in disbelief. His suit and tie really didn't fit here now. Ever.

"Like this?" she pointed at him and he took off his jacket, and his tie followed.

She laughed a little and wanted to tell him no. But at least he was here, ready to help her company and perhaps understand it all better. The more hands on deck, the better.

She explained where and how he could help. She thought that his literary knowledge would go down well indeed. And suddenly, he really did fit in super well here.

When her staff arrived, they looked at Lyle in amazement, but said nothing. Ally was particularly impressed and joined him. The two of them seemed to get along well, Mel thought to herself, but ignored her for the next couple of hours as all the families arrived one by one.

Lyle saw how she was absorbed in her work. She was the perfect hostess and gave everyone the joy of art. She inspired even the crankiest of parents, and always had a smile on her face ... even when *their* eyes met. Of course, that was only for the others, he knew. And yet her joy was his joy. He felt part of her passion.

It hit him all the more when her smile went out in an instant. He looked from her to the door where a young father was just entering with his son of perhaps eight years old. He had dark hair, was slim and quite attractive, in his eyes. He too saw Mel and a hot smile broke out on the latter's face. His desire for *her* was written right across his face, it was unmistakable, for Lyle had felt it all too often himself.

Lyle was sick with jealousy. He could only *imagine* exactly how these two knew each other. It was so blindingly blatant that even a blind man would see it. The two had been, or still were, *lovers*. He clenched his hands into fists. He had to do something, but was caught up in this stupid family day. He apologised to the children and was about to walk straight up to Mel and drag her out of the hall by the arm. He didn't get the chance, because she herself had already fled the hall without looking back.

Lyle was confused. He looked again at this man who still had a big smile on his handsome face. It was arrogant and provocative. Lyle's anger was overflowing.

He followed her into her office. She was about to grab her handbag. Her face was as white as a sheet. She was clearly driven by shame – and so she *should* be! Especially once *he* had finished with her.

She literally froze when she saw him in front of her. After only a second she composed herself and she tried to walk past him.

"I have to go." she said quickly. But Lyle grabbed her hard by the arm and stopped her from just running away.

"On such an important day?" he countered. It didn't escape him how she couldn't look him in the eye. She was trembling all over. "Is he your lover?"

Mel looked up into his face in shock. She felt sick as a dog.

Bull's-eye, he thought. *Disappointed.* He had hoped, after all, that she would at least deny it. But the guilt was written all over her face.

"Let go of me." she pleaded. She felt sick, her head was spinning and she could hardly breathe. She was on the verge of a panic attack. She didn't want to collapse in front of him here. She still had to make it to her home.

"Who else have you been sleeping around with? Now I see why you keep surprising me with this untamed passion. Have you gotten so used to your *active* sex life that you can't be without?"

Mel was speechless at his cold, callous accusations. Had he convinced himself of all this so he could hate her? Had he been looking for an excuse all this time why he didn't want to be near her anymore? Had he gone along with it all because he had really only been driven by this animalistic lust?

She jerked her arm free and stepped away from him. His eyes sparkled with hatred and revulsion. She didn't even know how to face it. Just knew she couldn't stay here any longer.

"This is all nonsense," she said weakly. But he did not hear her words at all. He was believing all of his ideas that nothing else mattered. What's more, she could only imagine what it looked like to him. Pale as a corpse and she wanted to escape.

"I don't even know you anymore. What happened here in the last few months? Am I making a total fool of myself in front of everyone? Are they laughing at me ... at us?"

Mel found one last bit of strength in herself. Some more fighting spirit.

"You're right about that, actually. You don't *know* me. Never took the *time* for *that*. Otherwise, you'd know exactly why I'm leaving now."

She didn't want to spend another second in his presence.

"Were you wearing your ring when you were screwing him?"

She ignored him, each word cutting into her heart.

As she walked past the hall, Ally came out to get her.

Mel was functioning only robotically. She had planned this day to the very last detail, had hoped for the best. Now it was all ruined. And she didn't cry anymore.

"Mel, we need - "

"I'm not well. Please, take care of the families. You can do it without me."

Stunned Ally looked after her boss and then at Lyle. It was obvious they had just had an argument. The chill was still in the air. She gave him a panicked look.

He took a deep breath. He wasn't simply going to let her go, had to talk to her. At the same moment, he couldn't turn his back on her company. It meant the world to her. Then he remembered what Mel had told him at the beginning. With his guidance and the eager employees, they brought the day to a successful end.

Every now and then his eyes wandered over to *the* father. Finally, he let his curiosity win out and he offered to help him too. That was after all why he was there, to *help*.

The man was extremely friendly and courteous, not at all ill-mannered and kind to his young son. Lyle could see why Mel must have liked him. That hurt nonetheless.

"It seems your son has thoroughly enjoyed his day here."

"Absolutely. I must admit, I had my doubts at first as to whether we could spend the whole day here. But Mel's got it all worked out."

Lyle gritted his teeth until it became uncomfortable. They really did know each other. He obviously had no idea who was standing in front of *him* though.

"She has." He had to force himself not to say anything wrong. "So you *know* Mel?"

His innocent tone must have been convincing enough, because the man continued to manipulate his paintbrush perfectly fine. But a small smile flitted across his lips, causing anger to rise in Lyle's throat again.

"You could say that, yes."

Lyle's throat almost tightened at his comment. He had to think of his marriage first and foremost, of the *show*. He wondered how many people he had told about the affair. Or if it was even still going on? Lyle was getting nervous. Was that why she had disappeared so quickly, was it not over and done with between them?

The little boy in front of them had finished his picture. He had the same dark hair and dark eyes as his father. He was so innocent in all this.

"Daddy, can we go now?"

The man nodded patiently at him.

"Soon, Alex. You know Mummy's picking us up at three. Then we'll go to McDonalds."

The joy was written all over his face. His father rolled his eyes as he looked at Lyle again, as if to say that it really was just an exception today, but a welcome one.

Lyle frowned. He was confused, bitterly disappointed and kind of sad. She was having an affair with a married man. A father. As nice and quiet as he seemed, that didn't suit her, did it? But he had heard it with his own ears, he *knew* Mel. He had seen the way he smiled when he thought of Mel. And he knew such a smile only too well, that lust in his gaze. An ice-cold shower went down his spine. Was that why she was so passionate towards him? Had this man taken away her inhibitions? Damn it, had Lyle been a match for him? Had he not been enough for her?

His thoughts were destroying him. He could not cope with this situation. He had to know the truth, no matter how destructive it was. This marriage could not break down because of it. He could forgive her for that, couldn't he? But now his feelings were still too raw. He was too bitter and *hurt* to seek her out.

"Mr McClory, thank you so much for your help! You have saved the day. I hope your wife gets better soon."
Lyle looked at the young woman in front of him. Ally was attractive, and very jolly and chipper.
"Why don't you join us for a drink to celebrate the success?" She looked at him hopefully. Her cheeks slightly flushed from the long events of the day.
Joshua and the others had done great work too. Lyle offered to pay for a cleaning company to take care of everything. So they could call it a day. They were all very excited about it.
Lyle hesitated for another moment before finally changing his mind and agreeing to the drink. He didn't have the strength to hear the truth yet.
It wasn't a bad ending to the day at all. Mel was really lucky, with the staff. They were reliable and above all motivated to really do their best for the children every day and today they had proved it once again. The mood was cheerful, despite a long day. They chatted about their plans for the rest of the weekend. Everything seemed so normal.
Lyle found himself with one or two too many glasses of beer in his hand and had Ally's full attention. He was only half listening to her. His thoughts were on Mel. He barely noticed Ally put her hand on his.
By the end of the evening his head was a little *clearer*, the alcohol had certainly helped. With the fresh air outside the pub came the desire to see her. He said her address as he climbed into the taxi, not quite as stable as usual. How much had he had to drink? He had few memories left of the evening. All he knew now was that he wanted to see her. As soon as possible.
Melissa knew it was him. Who else would be ringing her doorbell at this hour? She wanted to ignore him at first, wanted to just push the whole thing away, but she knew she would have to face him again sometime. It might as well be now.
She hadn't expected to see him so *drunk* in front of her. The stench of alcohol hit her first, his untidy clothes next. Had he got drunk because of her? Was she shocked or strangely moved?

Or both?

They probably wouldn't be able to have a clear conversation today. He needed a bed and to sleep it off.

He suddenly looked at her properly. Her heart stopped. Then the moment was over again.

"There you are. Alone, I hope."

"Lyle, do you want me to call you a taxi?" she asked sternly.

"You are my wife." he slurred when he saw her. He could barely hold himself up, his eyes half closed, half open. He stepped towards her. Mel stepped out of his way. She didn't want his proximity, not like this.

"If it's just sex you want, then I'm here for you anytime. You don't have to look for anyone else."

He tried to come closer again, and he was so quick that he managed to press his mouth to her lips. He tasted like beer, he smelled like a pub, even a sweet smell. She braced her hands against his chest. Considering he was barely able to stand, he had quite a bit of strength left in him. She couldn't push him off her so easily.

She turned her head as far as she could. His mouth landed on her neck. He became greedier and his hands went under her T-shirt and then to her waistband. Panic rose in her and she tried once more to twist out of his arms. He was not himself.

"Lyle." she pleaded.

Somewhere deep inside, he heard her and the pressure eased. He stared at her as if only seeing her at that moment. His hands fell away from her as if he had been burned. He took a step back and then another.

His look was shocked, at himself. He was at the end of his strength. He collapsed tired and broken on her sofa in front of him and fell asleep.

Mel still stood quivering in the same spot. Unsure of what had just happened. And what would happen now.

~ 130 ~

Melissa could not sleep a wink this night. The events of the previous day were weighing heavily on her conscience. And everything that was connected with it. She was also acutely aware that Lyle was sleeping on *her* couch and she couldn't avoid a conversation, confrontation with him. She didn't want to talk about it, but she also didn't want this oppressing atmosphere between them anymore.

She went to her kitchen to prepare breakfast. She rattled all kinds of plates and cups to wake him up. He didn't move an inch. With a loud bang, she placed a full plate in front of him on the small living room table and waited.

He lay on his stomach, his shirt all scrunched up, his trousers still on. How had he been able to sleep like that? Why had he drunk *so much*?

Lyle slowly opened his eyes. The bright light caused small stitches behind his eyes. He rose cautiously so that his world would stop spinning. He wasn't feeling well at all. He looked at Mel. Slowly, a few memories came back to him. Not many, but enough.

"Melissa, I'm sorry. I - " He shook his head, which was not a good idea. He had no words for what he had done. "I'm sorry I ambushed you so late at night."

She returned his gaze, not sure what *exactly* he was remembering. He seemed sincere. Had he calmed down again and they could talk about everything in peace?

"I can't share you." came his words and Mel swallowed dryly.

Her heart suddenly pounded to her throat and her hands grew clammy. She didn't believe her ears, was suddenly on edge. Was now the moment when he would finally tell her that he *did* have feelings for her? Was that why he had been so drunk, because of his heartache? Had it just taken some jealousy to show him how much he *loved* her?

Melissa felt the excitement rising deep inside her. She could hardly wait, and wanted to hear his voice, Melissa McClory, I love -.

"My sister ... "

Melissa dropped hard back onto earth. All her hopes blown away. Silly, dumb fantasies of a *girl*, nothing more. Nothing had changed, not one single thing. On the contrary, everything was a hundred times worse.

"My sister wants to ruin me. She will not, simply *will not* let our marriage rest until she finds something to prove that we are not *real*. Then legally she will get all the money my father has worked for all his life. She'd be wasting it all. She doesn't know how to handle money. She's living day to day. Man, I know she's just trying to spite him. And after your long absence ... we don't need any more doubt around our marriage. I've given every-thing I have to keep up appearances."

Melissa saw and knew how important it was to him that the inheritance did not go to her. She had never doubted that. Only today she didn't *care* at all. She couldn't be bothered with that right now.

"Eat something. Soak up the excess alcohol." she said coldly and stood up again.

He wasn't quite awake yet, but immediately sensed her mood. He ignored his stomach, and followed her into the small lean-to kitchen. His head began to pound.

"You – *you* are mad at *me*?" he asked so crossly. He remembered enough now why he hadn't refused a glass or two. "*You*'re the one who keeps putting *our* marriage at risk."

Mel sent him an evil glare. Her eyes sparked fire. Did he really feel up to an argument? Because she didn't.

"I don't want to talk about it. You're not listening to me any-way." she said coldly.

Lyle stood so close to her that he was able to grab her arm and turn her back to him.

"For fuck's sake, Mel. You're - "

"Your wife! As if I could ever forget that!" she interrupted him abruptly, jerking her arm free. She slipped away into the living room, needing to get out of his overwhelming proximity.

"Whatever have you been up to in the last few months? Who else will I meet that's had your attention?" He was really sick at the thought of how many men there must have been. All this time he had only worried about this *Roger* and now he realised how stupid he had actually been. She was an attractive woman, simply gorgeous. There were hundreds of men who would fall for her. Why hadn't he accepted that before? He knew first hand how seductive she was, how she could make you lose your self-control in an instance. He felt a painful tug in his heart, *ignored* it out of principle.

"I'm not having an affair with Ben."

Lyle stared at her.

"Ben?" He was shocked to the core. She was lying. She was lying to his face. "So you didn't sleep with him?"

Mel's face went pale. She felt her breath catch at the thought of him. Her expression portrayed everything, and really *nothing*. Lyle only saw the *guilt* written across her face and he ran a hand through his hair in utter despair.

"And you're still lying." He was so disappointed; she could see it in his eyes. "I can't even *look* at you."

"Then just go." she managed with difficulty. Her nerves were at breaking point. Her strength had long since run out. All she wanted was to be alone and wallow in self-pity.

Lyle's eyes were ice cold. His body stiff and unapproachable. He meant what he said. He couldn't stay here with her a second longer.

He grabbed his jacket and left her flat.

Melissa looked at the closed door for a long time. How had they once been so close? Had it really been the two of them in the hotel room? At the event?

How could they ever find their way back to each other? Or was it too late for that?

~ 131 ~

It was hard for her to let herself be seen at work again on Monday. Her guilty conscience had plagued her for hours. She would have preferred to stay at home for another day, but her mind told her that would not help *anyone*. Her employees would only start spreading gossip, which was unnecessary.

She was surprised at how neat and tidy everything was when she arrived. Ally greeted her kindly and nodded towards the rooms.

"Great, isn't it? Lyle paid for the cleaner and then for all the rounds! You have a great dancer for a husband. He moves effortlessly." Ally's eyes sparkled at her recollections and didn't even notice how Mel looked at her in shock. Had *she* spent the evening with her husband? And danced together as well? Was this a fucking joke?

"I hope you're feeling better," the young woman said in conclusion and walked off. It completely escaped her notice how pale Mel suddenly looked and rushed into her office in a hurry.

She leaned breathlessly against the door. All sorts of images came into her head. All unbearably painful. All with her young, sexy employee, in sensual embraces. Hot kisses.

Melissa literally shook and trembled all over. She didn't know how she could spend the next hours, days or even weeks here at work, working next to this woman. How could she ever concentrate on her work again? Everything seemed hopeless.

You are doing it for the *children*, that's why, spoke a strong voice in the back of her mind.

And only then did she pluck up courage again and begin her long day. Yes, for the children. They managed to distract her from her own worries without any problems. She had the strength to come back the next day and then again.

On Wednesday, she stood still, frozen in place. Lyle was equally surprised to see her so early. He had a cardboard box in his arm. She spotted the framed picture of herself within the box. A present she had once given him from their second reception. Momentarily, she felt touched. Then she remembered. He should*n't* be here so early with his *things*! He looked suspicious.

"I'm working here from now on." he finally explained after they just looked at each other in silence. Neither of them wanted to start first and clear the air.

"No." she said crassly. Her panic was written all over her face. "No, you are not."

"There's no longer any danger of me distracting you from your work." he replied coldly and Mel remembered her confession so long ago. Was that true too?

"I don't want you here. It's my business. Not the McClory show!" She was furious and beside herself with rage. What was he thinking? From the looks of it, he had already moved into one of the empty rooms. It all seemed pre-planned and arranged. She wanted to scream and snatch the things out of his hands. This is what this bloody photograph was for – to display a happy husband staring at a photograph of his beloved wife. Aaaargggghh-hhh!

"Too late. It will do our marriage good. At least the one on paper." he added coolly. "Our contract."

"Good? How is this going to be good for us?" She pointed to the two of them, and how they couldn't even talk peacefully for a few seconds.

"It's *expected*. People know I'm here too. However, they hardly see us together. Now is the time to spend more time together."

She shook her head in disbelief. She didn't care for a word he said.

"You want to see what I do all day," she countered coldly. "And with *whom*."

Lyle's eyes twinkled wickedly. That had been a deciding factor too.

"We need to repair the damage you've done." he said bitterly, stroking her cheek. It wasn't tender, it wasn't arousing, it was mocking. Melissa gritted her teeth.

"Or do you want to work closer with Ally?"

He laughed briefly, seeming genuinely amused at her remark. It was absolutely not the reaction she had expected. Relief spread, if he wasn't interested in her, it was a huge weight off her mind.

"You are my wife." he repeated himself for the twentieth time, suddenly looking at her strangely. He suddenly became all too aware of how close she stood in front of him. He felt her warmth. She had not smiled for a long time. She looked pale.

This time his touch was gentle and genuine. She felt her protective wall begin to crumble. "And I am your husband."

They just looked at each other in silence for a few seconds. So much remained unspoken. So much remained closed, kept secret. But in that moment, they were no longer arguing, and felt like a couple again. For those few seconds, their looks said it all.

"Good morning. Ah Lyle, moved in already?"

Ally's cheerful greeting brought her out of this spell again. Mel stepped away from him and went into her office. What would have happened if Ally hadn't turned up so suddenly? What had she wanted to have happened? What would Mel have allowed to happen?

They would both never have the answer.

~ 132 ~

Fortunately, she had her work. Her classes were popular and the children shone day after day. The monthly issue for the children's organisation and for her own company continued to be a great success. There were families who travelled miles to participate in her family days. Some stories were published in local newspapers.

Twice a week she had the incredible opportunity to draw with real cartoonists. Kurt had kept his promise. It was a great hit. The other writers she had approached at a few of the events also kept their word and gradually her business took on new heights. Melissa was so proud. She hardly noticed Lyle, who sat in his little office every day working on a new book, or whatever it was he was doing.

They stayed out of each other's way, completely.

She was fine. Everything was perfect. Almost perfect. The problem lay with Ben, or Benjamin Stokes, his full name. She stared blindly at the papers. Her hands were shaking.

He had signed himself and his son up for the family day again. The next day. She couldn't ask her staff to run it again. She couldn't be in the same hall as him. She was in an impossible situation. Could she cancel on him? But it was about his child after all. She had to put her own concerns aside and just let bygones be bygones. So much time had already passed. But her trembling hands and cramped stomach proved her wrong, that it hadn't long enough. She felt sick.

Mel made the decision to send him an email, professionally conveying her regrets that there was no more space. For her, the subject was closed.

To shake off her tension, she went to the kitchen to get a glass of water. Lyle was already there, holding a cup in his hand. She saw the wedding ring glint in the light. A stab in her heart.

Their eyes met. She ignored the tumult of emotions that suddenly stirred within her.

"Smile, Mel." he whispered in her ear as she stood beside him at the sink to fill her glass of water. She felt his hot breath on her skin. Deepest longing awoke in her. She just wanted to embrace him and feel his strong arms around her. She did not manage to smile right away. She suddenly felt so sad.

Lyle was not blind. He noticed her silence, was worried for her. But he hadn't forgotten how she could just lie to his face, without batting an eyelid. It was unforgivable. Unfortunately, he listened too little to his mind, and much more to his body. He ignored her strange demeanour.

"For our audience." he said softly before pressing his lips to hers, ever so gently and tenderly that it took her breath away. It had only been meant to be a brief kiss. To last only a moment, but that was not enough for him. He wanted more, so much more. No matter who she had been with, nothing mattered to him when he had her with him. So willing, so *innocent*.

He cursed the cup in his hand, wanted to touch Mel and pull her to him, but could hardly do it with one arm. He put his other hand possessively around her neck to press her mouth even closer to him. Meeting no resistance, he deepened his kiss. Soft noises came towards him. She was driving him crazy, he thought as he pressed her against the edge of the kitchen counter. He had to pull back; this show had completely gotten out of hand.

Mel was slow to open her eyes. Had lost herself completely in the kiss, only to look into his cold eyes now. She was back to reality. Was disappointed and *humiliated*.

She ignored her weeping heart and returned his cold stare instantly.

"Next time at least have the guts to go through with it. For your audience."

With those words, she left him standing. Her legs carried her reliably to her office, but no further. Her heart was beating up to her throat. She had fallen at his feet again, completely and utterly. What was wrong with her?
It was only a matter of time before she would lose control again and wake up in his bed. It was inevitable. Her heart would break again *and again* as long as he was in her life.

~ 133 ~

It got worse and worse. After one well-intended email, she received a response. Every day, every hour. Each time just a few words, short statements.

Melissa tried blocking his address. It didn't help. They kept coming through.

Remember us?

Fuck me again.

You bitch.

Useless.

Unsatisfying.

Waiting for you.

Melissa pushed the fear and panic from her thoughts and put all her focus on her classes. She didn't have much time to worry during the day. It was only in the evening, when twenty or thirty emails awaited her, that she was reminded that Ben was trying to get her back into his games. She ignored them as best she could. But she was nervous and jaded.

He knew where she worked, could call on her any time he wanted to. He had the power.

The phone rang and Melissa welcomed the distraction. She smiled into the receiver, even though no one could see her.

The smile froze on her face when no one answered. Instead, only obscene noises came from the other end. Shocked and afraid, she hung up.

Melissa nearly jumped out of her skin as Lyle stepped into her office. He recognised panic on her face.

"Are you all right?"

"Yes.... of course." She lied. The last thing she wanted to do was mention his name in front of him. Lyle didn't believe a word she said. She looked worn-out, wasn't like herself at all.

"We're having dinner with Angela and Kurt tomorrow."

Mel didn't respond to his remark. She had not the slightest interest in spending an evening with his acquaintances. She preferred to be alone in her flat, all doors and windows locked.

"I'll pick you up."

No response. She looked silently out her windows; it was already dark. All of a sudden, she felt uneasy. Her phone rang.

"Lyle, wait." She jumped up as he was already leaving. He was surprised. She grabbed her purse and left everything else. The phone continued to ring. He had never seen her do that before. Ignore her business? What was wrong with her?

She stayed by his side until they stood in front of the business building. Her car was a little further away, but she didn't dare ask him to go with her.

She made it to her car in one piece and without any problems. She was angry with herself that she had let her fear get so out of control that she was now seeing ghosts everywhere. It was only Ben after all. Yes, he wrote her a few childish emails. He was doing exactly what he used to do. That's all it had been. No fear to panic or to expect anything worse to come. She was just imagining things. He was married now, had a small child. He was completely harmless.

It wasn't until she was in the car that she saw the note on her wing mirror.

"I see you."

~ 134 ~

For the first time in this *world*, she wished a dinner would last longer. She did her best to talk openly and good-naturedly with Kurt, also ignoring every cold pointed remark that came from Angela. Most of all, she didn't let Lyle leave her side. As soon as the evening was over, he would drop her back at home and she panicked slightly at the thought of being alone for the night and the next day.

She grabbed the glass of wine that was in front of her and drank it down in one go. Lyle noticed, knowing that she never actually drank. Unless...

After saying goodbye to the others, they stood motionless in front of the taxi. The September air had turned rather chilly; Mel covered herself with her thin jacket.

Lyle turned to her. His gaze was cold and closed.

In her distress at not being able to cope alone this night, she acted from her heart.

He *had* expected her kiss, nonetheless he was instantly on fire. Her lips were soft and sugary sweet. Because she had been drinking, and he knew very well that she was not *herself* then. It took all his strength to refuse her.

"Mel, what's the matter with you? You're all agitated."

Mel looked at him hurt. How had he been able to *resist* her? Had he lost his interest in her? Did she leave him cold?

The alcohol had loosened her senses somewhat. Her mind objected ever so slightly.

"Ben - "

Momentarily his expression darkened and she regretted even considering telling him. Well, telling him anything was out of the question now. Lyle wasn't showing the best listening skills at this moment.

"You're trying to seduce me and you're thinking about your Ben?"

He was shocked. He gave her a little push that she was more distant from him. She felt anger burning inside her. He was incorrigible. Had no idea what kind of person she was or he would *never* be able to imply that about her.

"No, I don't want to be alone."

His laugh was so cutting, it sent an icy chill down her spine. She had chosen her words wrong. It didn't help. The evening was ruined.

"You didn't have to be. *You left me.*" he replied honestly, stroking exhaustedly through his hair. This comment disturbed her and him much, much more than anticipated. "I need time."

Lyle opened the door of the taxi and waited for her to get in. That was it.

~ 135 ~

Melissa ignored the eighty-five emails on Monday morning. She gave her all to showing the children how art could help them. She found her passion and love when she painted with them. Painting was the best medicine, she thought, smiling at the children.

The last class of the day said goodbye to her. Once again, they had shown great talent, but most important joy. The beaming on their faces was their reward.

"Alex, did you have a good time?"

Mel wanted to run, wanted to scream. Instead, she stood frozen two metres away from *him*. He smiled kindly at her; his son hugged him warmly. *Shit.*

"Mel, it's good to see you again." His voice was friendly and warm. His gaze attentive and fixed on her. But his smile.... his smile seemed arrogant and far too confident, as if to say, Go on then, challenge me. "Are you not well?"

Mel's face had lost its colour and she had yet to get a word out. She felt trapped, unable to escape her own feelings. What was wrong with her? Her mind was active but her body was not responding. She felt like she had all those years ago. *Helpless.* She didn't believe in herself, believed *him*.

Wake up, Melissa! Remember who you *are* now!

"Too bad family days are always booked up." He said innocently now. He was hinting towards her email, his responses. She knew it. He *mustn't* win this game.

She was stronger than him. She was no longer *his* Mel.

"Yes, they are for the foreseeable future." she finally replied. Her voice was clear and distinct. Hang in there. The first step had cost her more than she'd thought.

"Luckily, there are a few other classes Alex likes."

She gritted her teeth. Why wasn't he leaving already? What else did he want?

"Alex, go ahead. I'll be right there."

Mel panicked. Now there were only the two of them. She had to get out of here. She set about passing him and fleeing the room. Ben was quicker.

"I'm surprised how far you've come. You were always so clumsy and useless." His voice was quiet but clear. Mel shivered, hearing every word. "Even now. Has the cat got your tongue? Can't get a word out. You weak link."

She looked at him bitterly. She had learned. Had learned to fight back, only somehow, he brought out the old Mel and she felt inferior and small. Damn it. *Damn it.*

"You are no longer wanted here." she replied forcefully.

Benjamin smirked.

"The way I see it, these classes here are for everyone. For *all* the children. Mine included."

She turned towards the door and had almost managed to get out of his reach.

"How old would our child be now? Eleven? Twelve?"

Melissa found the strength to flee the room, ran blindly into her office and locked herself in. She cried tears she hadn't cried in a long time. Felt pain and regret she hadn't felt in a long time. Her past had caught up with her again today. And it hurt just as much as it had twelve years ago. She didn't cry anymore, hadn't she said as much?

But these tears were for her innocent baby.

~ 136 ~

Melissa forced herself to stay at work. She forced herself to go home, alone. She forced herself not to break down. One more time. And then again.

She made it to work, ignoring the phone calls and emails. They meant nothing. She was not a failure. She wasn't hopelessly useless. She wasn't a bitch.

She needed to get on with her life. Benjamin no longer had any hold on her, on her life. She *had* achieved all this, everything. She was a successful illustrator. She was that. No matter what he said. No, she couldn't let him bring her to her knees. This was *it*. Enough.

She grabbed a pencil and began to draw. Within a few minutes, her mind had calmed down. Her thoughts were free. She drew without a plan, just from her thoughts. Until two cold eyes looked at her. Her stability, her hope, her present life.

She had to talk to him, whatever the cost. This rift between them had to be healed. Benjamin had almost destroyed their marriage, it had to stop. If she told him everything, surely, he *would* forgive her. Then he wouldn't be so cold towards her, then maybe they could talk or be in the same room with each other again. It had to be sorted out. *Today*.

She was glad that he worked here now. So she knew where to find him and didn't need an excuse to seek him out. And she didn't have the opportunity to change her mind.

He had followed all rules, he left her alone and he didn't mix his business with hers. Especially not lately, he hardly paid any attention to her, all because of this misunderstanding. She couldn't wait to have it all explained and to see the relief in his eyes. She wanted him to see her as his *wife* again. Not as this unfaithful person who, in his mind, was making passes at everyone and anyone.

Melissa put the pictures all aside. She would continue sorting them tomorrow. Today was the end of the day. Now was the right time to do it. It was quiet, without the children in the rooms.

She went straight to his office without even knocking.

A mistake. Or fate?

Her world shattered. Into a thousand pieces at her feet.

"Lyle..."

She didn't see much, not all of it, but she saw Ally put her arms around his neck and kiss him. She had seen *that* before she rushed out of the office and ran down the hundred flights of stairs without slowing down for a second. Breathless, she stopped on the ground floor.

How could she have been so bloody stupid? Why had she still hoped that he could *love* her? Why had she believed that he would keep their marriage vows? Even after so *long*. Of course, he had been lonely, had been disappointed in her and had only assumed the worst of her. But did he have to run to the next one? Then, on top of that, her employee who was more than ten years younger than her? Was she worth so little to him?

Mel breathed in and out deeply. In her blind shock, she had run out of the office without her bag or keys. She couldn't drive or walk home. It was too far. Although it was tempting. She couldn't believe she had reacted so childishly and not thought it through. Her shock turned to *anger*, at herself, at him, at Ally. How dare she make a pass at *her* husband?

With every step she angrily climbed, her fury grew.

She had wanted to *talk* to him. Finally wanted to clear the air and give them another chance. But no, he had to have his ways with a beautiful, *slim* 20-year-old. What had she been saying to herself an hour ago? It couldn't get any worse, could it? You're such a fucking idiot.

Now it was. And all because of that disgusting Benjamin Stokes.

She didn't give a damn how stupid it looked now that she appeared on her office floor again. She wouldn't grant him a word, get her bag and make an exit for the second time. She just hoped they weren't still together in his office. The thought of it almost broke her in two.

But they weren't. In fact, there was no sign of Ally. Lyle, on the other hand, was standing at her desk, his face full of anger. His eyebrows furrowed deeply.

Well, he could bloody do one if he thought to have the right to be angry with *her*. Now it was *her* turn.

"What's this? What are those degrading emails to you?"

Mel stopped as if struck. She hadn't expected *this*. He was staring at her. There wasn't just anger in his gaze, concern too. But that wasn't the point at all now. What was he thinking trying to distract from his misstep? She was going to have a go at him, not the other way around!

"What are you doing on my computer?" she deflected from his question and pressed the button on the screen to turn it off. Far too late, she realised. He had read enough, more than she probably had. "What are you doing in my office?"

"Your phone hasn't stopped ringing." he replied directly and far too calmly, holding her gaze. He knew full well she knew *what* he was talking about. Her reaction confirmed his suspicions. He was speechless for the moment. And then angry again. "How long have these obscenities been going on?"

Mel was silent. She was struggling with herself, wanting to reawaken her own anger. Didn't want to talk about herself, but about him and his sexy girlfriend. Oh, that hurt, thinking about her like that.

"Melissa! Talk to me." He was impatient and had no understanding that she hadn't said *a word* to him. Or had she? Had she tried to tell him what was going on? And he had turned her down? The night after dinner - had he been too stubborn, and refused her help?

"It's that guy. Benjamin. Ben. Isn't it?" He put his hands on her arms and searched her gaze. She stood stone-still. He shook her gently, feeling the despair rise within him. What had he done? Why hadn't he seen it? "Is he blackmailing you for sex?"

Melissa finally snapped out of her trance and freed herself from his grip, her eyes cold and full of hatred. His ideas of her had not changed at all. How was it possible that he could assume, even for a second, that she could have the *slightest* interest in another man? After all, she had told him that she had not wanted *anyone* for years. She felt more betrayed about that realisation than his kiss with Ally.

"You bastard!" she brought out between her teeth. She knew no deeper anger, no greater disappointment. "For the very last time, we are not having an affair. He is not a threat to our *staged* marriage." She had raised her voice, knowing she would lose her composure as soon as she had done so. She didn't care so much now. This was not a topic she wanted to discuss *again*. He didn't know her one bit. Did she know *him*? "Like you even care. What are you doing sticking it to Ally?"

To her great annoyance, she felt hot tears in her eyes. Banished them to her very core. She *did not* cry!

Lyle was totally confused. Believed her all of a sudden, wanted to make everything right. Wanted to turn back time, so that he could have helped her. Those emails were sick and would drag anyone down. How long had he been pestering her with his calls? Bloody hell, what was going on here?

"Ally?" He had pushed that moment completely aside. It had no meaning, had slipped his mind entirely. "We have more important things to discuss than that."

"No, absolutely not, we don't. We do not." she objected vehemently. She was quivering physically. Wanted to scream and make him hear and understand every word. "You've been avoiding me for weeks. Making me feel your deepest repulsion whenever I'm near you. All because of your wild, ill-founded fantasies about Ben. I'm not a bitch. I don't screw around. Don't you *know that*?"

This stress from the last few days, weeks, was coming to a head. She no longer had the strength to hide anything. Let him see her

true feelings. She couldn't help loving him. Her anger drove her.
"Mel - "

"No, now I'm talking." She didn't give him a chance. Was too upset to listen to him. Too disappointed, too sad, too broken. "You made it clear how *little* you think of me. And then I see *you* with *her*. And you had to have your own back. In front of my eyes. With her, a young... *slender... beauty*."

She shook her head, desperate and lost. He wanted to reach for her, wanted to hold her. But she rejected him.

"Don't touch me." She stepped as far away as she could. "Don't ever touch me again."

She grabbed her bag, what she had come for, and this time took the lift down. She knew he would not follow her.

~ 137 ~

Or would he?

The door opened again and Lyle joined her in the lift.

"Did you really think I would just let you go?"

Lyle was right in front of her. For a moment she felt like she was in one of her favourite novels. In which, one had been eagerly reading towards this moment, after all. He had come after her and all that was missing was all of her forgiveness and the most heart-warming happy ending with a declaration of endless love. But his very proximity, his arms around her, just before the moment of a passionate kiss, reminded her painfully of *what* she had seen. All she could think of was Ally, how she had been just as close to him, and that had been less than an hour ago. Her heart broke again and she lowered her head.

"All I see is you with *her*. I can't get it out of my mind."

Lyle dared to touch her. He lifted her head with his fingers. The lift door closed quietly behind them. It was going down, downhill, far too fast.

"Now you see how I felt."

"So you just wanted to get back at me?"

Her look was hurt.

"I have absolutely no interest in her. None. I don't even know why she tried to kiss me." he replied seriously. His body so close, was still so perfectly warm and inviting. "I only want you. We've lost so much time because of that sick guy. You're my - "

Mel didn't hear the rest of his words, leaning willingly towards his kiss. Her whole body awoke in that moment, her heart *opening* again. What more did she want to hear? This was almost like a declaration of *love* after all.

"The thought of you with him almost killed me." he whispered hastily and breathlessly before kissing the side of her neck.

Melissa came back to her senses and braced her hands against his chest.

"We need to talk about this." She tried bravely.

He kissed her neck, her ear, her cheek.

"You weren't having an affair. I believe you."

Again, she lost herself in his kiss, in his tenderness. She felt all the stress and worry from the last few weeks fall away from her. Her legs were soft, her body literally trembled. She also believed, in this moment, in his words. She heard much *more* than he had said. Hoped for more feelings for eternity, but he hadn't sworn them to her yet.

Lyle didn't let go of her as he looked at her kindly. Her eyes were dark but tired.

"I want nothing more than to lose myself in you." he said softly stroking her face. "But for today, I'll leave it at that."

Lyle saw her look at him in panic. He hated that look in her eyes, wanting to protect her and do everything he could to make her smile again.

"I'll stay with you, tonight. Tomorrow." He affirmed to her and she exhaled in relief.

They hadn't even noticed how the lift had long since reached the ground floor. How time had flown, in his safe arms.

Lyle took her hand. They had held hands before, but only for others. Today it seemed real and she smiled at him.

When they arrived at her car, she was too slow to remove the latest note from her wing mirror. Lyle tore it off angrily.

"Sleep tight." He gritted his teeth and jerkily looked all around. He wanted to do something. This all had to end. "Since when? How many times? Never mind. We'll go to the police, file a report."

Mel put her hands on his chest and kissed him. Before he could speak on, she had distracted him from his anger and he instantly lost control again. She loved his passion, enjoyed feeling his insatiable desire, as she did inside herself. It was incredibly arousing to know that she could do this to him in an instance. She alone, his *wife.*

"Take me home."

Lyle rested his forehead against hers and struggled to catch his breath, to clear his head. She was all he saw, all he wanted. He had no choice but to do as she said.

In the car they had enough time to calm their senses first and to indulge in their own thoughts a little. Arriving at her flat, they stood uncomfortably in the living room, which felt so small again.

"We need to talk things over and ... plan." He finally said.

Mel nodded.

"Where are you going to sleep?" she asked quietly.

"Best here, on the couch." He gestured to the small sofa and then grinned at her again. "That should be enough distance between me and you. I don't think I could bear a whole night next to you."

Mel ignored his choice and pulled his head down to her.

"And you think I can?" Her lips were hot, so hot that he responded to them instantly. He had missed her so much, had thought of her so much, had wished for this moment so many times. Now she was right in front of him, willing, but also exhausted, mentally drained. He had to remind himself of all she had been through, today and the last few weeks. He wouldn't, *couldn't* take advantage of her feelings like that. He had to keep his control. But her hands went into his hair, under his shirt, over his chest. His hands had taken on the same independence and were on her bottom, pressing her closer. He was close to ignoring his mind. Wanting to enjoy it just a second longer.

"Melissa McClory." he spoke in a hoarse voice, his lips millimetres from hers. His eyes as dark as hers. "You do what I tell you. Let's go to sleep and start the day fresh tomorrow. I want you all to myself, not sad, not restless and tormented or jealous. I want *my wife.*" Another soft kiss, a long breath. "Tomorrow."

He pushed her gently away from him, glad that for the first time she did as she was told without objections.

There was no end to this night, but at least they felt comfortable in each other's presence again after such a long time.

<h1 style="text-align:center">~ 138 ~</h1>

Lyle was on his mobile phone when she came into the living room. It was only seven o'clock in the morning, but she had not been able to wait any longer. She had been immensely aware all night that he had been sleeping on her couch. Just a few feet away from her and he had *wanted* her. Had said the nicest things to her, that she was on cloud nine.

He saw her coming towards him. He was wearing only his underwear, which he regretted at that moment. She had at least put on a bathrobe. Her hair fell softly and unruled over her shoulders. She looked ravishing. He had a hard time concentrating on his phone call.

His eyes went wide when she didn't stop as expected, and kept coming towards him. She put her hands on his chest and began kissing his neck, then his nipples.

Lyle drew in his breath loudly.

"Yes. ... Ah... I mean, no. I didn't forget." he stammered as she continued with her caresses. "Mmmmh, yes... ah... I remember. See you later."

Lyle hung up hastily and tossed his phone towards the sofa. He grabbed her hands to stop her, move her away slightly to get back some distance between them. What she was causing in him was becoming more and more obvious.

"What are you doing to me?"

"Today is tomorrow." she replied smiling, her eyes large and clear. She was no longer depressed or confused at all. She knew exactly what she wanted and when. "I am your wife...am I not?"

She stood on her tiptoes to whisper in his ear, grazing the side of his face with her lips, feeling his hard body against her. She knew how he fought with composure and she had already given up that attempt herself.

"We still need to talk." He said weakly as her hands ran down his back to his bottom and she leaned against him.

"I promise."

Lyle didn't stand a chance. This long time without her had taken a toll on his willpower. He had to have her, just had to. He took control and grabbed her hands, spinning her away from him so that Mel looked at him, puzzled. His gaze was dark, his breathing so staggered. She wasn't sure why he suddenly didn't want her near him, began to doubt herself as he pushed her passionately against her wall, kissing her so deeply that her legs gave way. As if he knew this, he held her securely in his grip, robbing her of all her senses. A hot sound escaped her as he pushed hard against her, aroused. He let go of her hands, and skilfully, slipped the dressing gown off her body, only to see that she was naked underneath. She was so beautiful, so perfect for him.

"Oh Mel." He was breathless, he wasn't close enough to her.

Mel had her arms back and was doing the same to him, lightly brushing the last bit of fabric from their bodies so that nothing stood between them. At last. Again.

<h1 style="text-align:center">~ 139 ~</h1>

"That hadn't been the plan," he said softly into her neck. They both struggled for breath and could hardly believe what had just happened.

Mel smiled and gave him a light kiss on the cheek. Her face was slightly flushed from her ecstasy. She felt fabulous.

"We should get dressed for our conversation." she suggested.

Lyle played playfully with her nipple, making her feel that familiar tug in her stomach. Why talk? Being here together was a thousand times better. They could just stay here, and love each other. It was *love*, wasn't it?

"Mmmmh." was his reply. He didn't seem to hear her. His attention was focused on her breasts. Mel felt his tongue leave a hot trail. She made small, sweet noises of happiness.

It wasn't until much later that they found themselves at her high table that separated the en suite kitchen to the front room. Both on either side to keep at least some distance between them. They had showered, made love, dressed and were now finally sitting across from each other ready to put everything on the table. *Shit.*

For a fleeting moment she panicked, wondering if he could actually handle the truth, and then she remembered his words. He wanted her, only her. That meant he *loved* her too and could certainly bear her past. She had waited far too long to tell him everything, it just had to happen. Surely, he wouldn't turn his back on her again, not after they had just spent the most breathtaking hours together.

"So why is this guy bothering you?"

Mel sat down on the other side of the counter, holding her cup in her hands. Lyle had spoken first, and naturally wanted to get straight to the point. That was understandable. But as much as she had wanted to tell him, she didn't know how to explain everything so that he wouldn't pull away from her again. That he didn't counter with his cold front, which made her life difficult and broke her heart.

"You know why I agreed to marry you?"

Lyle looked at her a little confused and impatient. Why was she diverting from the subject? Hadn't they wasted enough time?

"Because of the inheritance." was his first reply, seeing her horrified expression on her face. "Because we both have no interest in long-drawn-out relationships and are old enough to know that true love doesn't exist." He continued.

Mel agreed with him, at least with half of it. But those *were* the very reasons. She had never wanted to fall in love again. Had had no interest in men, in many, many years. Had looked forward to financial security in life. Unfortunately, all those plans went down the drain the moment she had fallen head over heels in love with Lyle. But they would have to talk about *that* another time.

"Ben is the reason." she finally said, noticing how he had to process this answer first. She didn't give him too much time to think about what that meant before she continued. "He was my first great love. I was eighteen, totally blown away by this twenty-year-old who was courting me. He was attentive, funny, decent.... *Everyone* found him so polite and outgoing. They couldn't say a bad word about him. They only knew him as the *perfect* gentleman."

She felt her hands shaking, it ran ice cold down her spine as she thought back to those days. She avoided those memories as much as she could, not letting the feelings of disappointment get to her. But the pain came up again. And the disbelief that he could have done all that to her.

"He ..." She crossed her arms in front of her chest, as if that would protect her from what she was saying. She looked pale, shaky. "Once we were alone, he was a completely different person. He put me down, talked badly about my drawings. Laughed at everything I set out to do. He just made fun of me. Over and over again. Everything I did was not good enough, *ever*. I'm useless and I'll never amount to anything."

Lyle noticed how she had slipped into the present tense, wanted to interrupt her, but she didn't see him. Was caught up in her own world, in those terrible memories.

"He exerted such power over me, it was incredible. He insulted my body, everything about me, he hated having sex with me and at the same moment he would force himself on me until I couldn't take it anymore."

She felt sick at the thought, at his breath on her face, at his hands around her neck. She stood up abruptly and got herself something to drink. She now looked as white as a sheet.

"He ruined my confidence, my belief that I was good enough for anything, anybody. He was excelling at these ongoing mind games."

"Melissa, for how long, I mean, why ..." He didn't know how to ask his questions all at once. She could see in his face that he couldn't understand how she had stayed with him. Why she hadn't sought help.

"I believed him. For months. For two years." she answered honestly.

"How could he do such a thing to you? For years? Thank God you found yourself." He did not move away from her, but sought her closeness, grasping her arms to show her he was there for her. But she feared he would not stay there. Still, she didn't want to keep anything a secret. Not anymore.

"I would have stayed with him." she admitted sadly. Her heart contracted painfully. "I was pregnant."

Lyle let go automatically, had not expected it, had not prepared for it and therefore had no appropriate reaction. She had suspected it. She couldn't blame him. Wouldn't know how she would react to it herself either, if it were his past.

He involuntarily took a step back. His thoughts and feelings in total turmoil.

"I wanted to keep the child, wanted to give him the love I lacked. Ben saw only one more way of constantly putting me down. For months. I wouldn't be a good mother; I was basically inept and the baby wouldn't stand a chance. I... drank, he stirred up more hatred against me. A fight broke out, I woke up in hospital ... and the baby was gone."

She felt sick. Her body stiff and cold. She hadn't thought about that night for years. As much as she had lost then, in that lonely room, she had gained with it.

She took a deep breath.

"I found the courage to leave him, started a degree, worked on children's stories here and there as an illustrator. The rest is ... history."

Lyle hadn't moved an inch. His gaze unmoving and unreadable. She had wanted to be honest, and she had been. Now she was paying the price. It served her right. She should have told him something as major as that at the beginning.

"It's perfectly clear to me that you don't want to be with me now. I can understand that."

He shook his head slowly, taking a moment to regain his composure.

"You're not useless, you're not a disappointment. Look at what you've achieved. Your children want to be like you. *All* of your children."

He kissed her cheeks, held her tightly in his arms, protected her.

"If I ever see him again ..." he finally murmured to himself, making Mel grin. She was so happy at that moment, felt so free. Why hadn't she told him a long time ago? He was right, far too much time had been lost.

"Are you going to punch him in the nose, like Richard?"

They both laughed lightly at the thought of his heroism. It seemed ages since he had protected her from that alky. So much already connected them, their marriage was so strong. But he became serious again and looked her in the eye.

"So that's why it's a no to children?" His tone serious and sincere. He seemed to really understand her.

She nodded slightly. She couldn't get over it if she lost another baby.

"Then we did exactly the right thing with our marriage. Am glad we both feel the same way. Don't give love a chance."

He laughed and gave her a kiss.

Melissa suddenly didn't feel like laughing. More like crying.

Lyle didn't notice her silence, and glanced fleetingly at his watch.

"Before I forget again, we have a date tonight. We're going to the theatre. A sponsor of my new book has invited us. It's going to be dead boring, but with you by my side, in a dark auditorium, it's suddenly going to be much more delightful."

She smiled after him as he disappeared into the bathroom. They had taken two steps forward, and five steps back.

After all these revelations, all these passionate hours, there was no declaration of love on his part after all. In fact, it was only attraction after all. Melissa wanted to go lick her wounds, wanted to be alone, but Lyle had other ideas.

Fortunately, her body was just as attuned to him, and within seconds he managed to distract her completely from her negative thoughts.

~ 140 ~

To be honest, she was looking forward to this visit to the theatre. She hadn't had the chance to go to one since her wedding and today was one of her favourite plays. Apart from that, Lyle was by her side. He was attentive and confident, just as she needed him to be. He looked stunning in his outfit. If she didn't already love him, she would fall in love with him all over again. Mel stopped him from going into the theatre and pulled him close to her. She paid no attention to the looks of the others, cared not for the women who looked at her shaking their heads. She ignored the many unspoken taboos. She felt his warmth infuse her, felt the desire deep inside *him*. Once again, it made her feel quite powerful to know that he was responding to her like this. Just her, the normal woman, without glamour or extras. It was *incredible*.

"I could be super easily persuaded to take you back to your place right now." he murmured into her neck, his hands stroking seductively down her back, down to her bottom.

"Later." she promised him with a gleam in her eye.

They broke away from each other with difficulty and walked towards the entrance.

Fuck.

There stood Benjamin, with his arm around a slender beauty. Her warm feelings in her stomach instantly forgotten, and a deep lump replaced them instead.

Mel's heart sank with a thud, she felt Lyle tense beside her and then take a firm step towards the couple. She had no idea what he was up to, feared the worst. She wanted to stop him, stop him from making a scene here in front of everyone. She felt sick and her legs were shaking.

"Lyle..." she asked softly but insistently, but in his fury, he didn't hear her.

Ben recognised her first, then saw the man at her side. His smile was put on, but his eyes moved nimbly back and forth, from her to *his* wife and then back to Lyle. He saw immediately that Lyle knew *everything.* He straightened his shoulders and braced himself for a blow.

"What a lucky coincidence to meet here. Did you enjoy our family day with your son *Alex*?" said Lyle kindly with an underlying cold tone.

The woman at his side looked a little puzzled at first and then she remembered, the drawings her son had brought home. She gave them a friendly smile. She didn't seem to notice the tension. Until she suddenly recognised him.

"Benny, I can't believe it, that's Lyle McClory. Oh my God, you met him? You're my absolute favourite writer."

She was so excited and held out her hand. Lyle politely accepted it and returned her kindness. *She* was not the problem; her husband was the perverted type who was bullying his own wife.

"I worked with your son one afternoon when he was with my wife in our children's classes. He told me so much about you. He is a very special, bright little boy. He's in the third grade at Kurt Baldauf Primary School, isn't he?"

Ben heard the warning in Lyle's remarks, and narrowed his eyes slightly.

"Wife?" he barely managed to get out. That hadn't escaped him.

Mel ignored his question and spoke with the same candour and friendliness as Lyle. "In fact, you and I were just talking about Alex. He has shown such talent in the many times he has been there. His teacher Mrs Tenant will be very impressed."

This time the woman looked a little more surprised and sent a questioning look to her husband.

Ben ignored her and just shrugged.

"He wasn't so keen on it himself." he tried to put her down indirectly. But Lyle didn't let him continue. His friendliness had subsided and his eyes were cold and insistent.

"Melissa, why don't you go ahead with Ben's escort. They are already waiting for us to enter."

She gave him another quick look without revealing her concern in her gaze. Then she walked off with his wife. She seemed so nice and innocent in the whole situation. She wanted to ask her if he made her *happy*. But she stopped herself from doing so. Maybe it was completely different with her, maybe he had found his *fulfilment* in her.

"I can't believe Alex worked with Lyle McClory. Your company is a fantastic idea to give young kids a springboard."

Mel smiled sweetly and nodded at her.

"I do everything for my children so they believe in themselves. *No one* should ever feel like they're not good enough for something. *Everyone* has their own spark and that should be nurtured and never extinguished."

The woman agreed with her. Her eyes were warm and sincere. Mel saw no worries or suffering. She was content.

A few minutes later the men approached them again. Lyle gave Mel a light kiss on the mouth. He wanted to show that she was his and she welcomed it.

Benjamin, on the other hand, looked a little pale and without further ado he apologised to them both and pulled his wife back with him towards the car park. They would attend the play another time.

Mel stared at her husband.

"No brawl?"

"Just one or two clarifications made. He seemed *very* understanding."

She felt the adrenaline leave her limbs. She gripped his arms to keep her footing. He took her in a safe, protective embrace.

"I had a great desire to beat the living daylight out of him. We shouldn't let him get away with it so easily."

She looked up at him, his gaze cool and distant, but not because of her. He continued to look after her ex-boyfriend for a long time. He was sure she wouldn't hear from him again and yet he

had to see it with his own eyes as he disappeared into the distance. He would make other permanent arrangements also.
"Thank you, Lyle."
He turned his attention back to her. This time his expression was warm and loving. Her heart blossomed.
After a deeply moving long kiss, they finally found their way into the theatre. Only a few people noticed their tardiness, but ignored it. To her, it looked as if the two had lost track of time. She felt the cold stares that came her way from the other women. Today she felt stronger than ever to fit into this world, with him by her side.

The play had been touching. The night had been fulfilling. Sunday had been intense. Mel couldn't remember when she had felt so good and not a fight in sight *any*where. Now it was the beginning where they would treat each other respectfully and in time she would get *him* to fall in love with *her*. It couldn't turn out any other way.

Mel heard the knocking from far away. She had been sound asleep just then, wrapped in his strong arms, his face pressed into her hair. They had even made it to her bed this time. What a night.

She grabbed her dressing gown and ran to the door as the knocking grew louder.

"Mel. Wake up."

It was her friend Patty. So early in the morning? Well, that was a surprise.

She opened the door, whereupon the woman immediately entered and thrust a newspaper into her hand.

"Did you finally sign the divorce papers?"

Mel was confused. She hadn't expected such a greeting. The thought of a divorce had completely slipped her mind. If her friend knew who was in her bed right now ....

"Read it."

Mel looked obediently at the newspaper she held in her hand. A soft curse escaped her before she sat down on the armchair, mute and shocked.

The first thing she saw was a dark, blurry image of Lyle and Ally together. Blurry, but clear enough to see that it was him, in a bar with her. His arm around her shoulders.

Then the headline. "Hot date with successful *married* writer Lyle McClory".

Mel's face went pale, her hands shook, she felt sick to the stomach.

Allison had gone to a tabloid with her *believable* story and they had printed it within two days. I guess they hoped to interest enough readers and didn't care whose hearts and illusions they broke in the process. Like her own, and the illusion that their marriage could have been real.

Ally talked mostly about one particular night, with him in the pub, where he obviously hadn't been able to resist her. She also mentioned a kiss at his workplace where he had not offered the slightest resistance. If his wife hadn't come to pick him up from work, she doesn't know how it would have *ended.*

Mel closed the newspaper. She needed to think clearly.

"See? He's destroying you. He's totally making fun of you. Who knows what else goes on behind your back? That's why he's never there for you. Mel, you need to draw a line."

"Melissa?"

Lyle stood half-naked in the living room, leaving her friend in no doubt as to what had happened here. Patty stood up abruptly.

"She deserves more. You disgusting, cheating scoundrel."

Lyle didn't have the chance to defend himself in any way. With these cold words she left the flat without a second glance.

He stared at her in bemusement and Mel handed him the newspaper. He cursed angrily and threw it on the living room table.

"That brat." He looked up and noticed that Mel had not yet said a word. When he tried to touch her, she avoided him.

"Mel, this is all nonsense. You know that."

"No, Lyle. I don't *know* that." she countered, pointing to the picture. "That picture was taken the night you came to my flat drunk as a skunk. You were completely out of it, your clothes all messed up, your hair dishevelled. What really happened that night?"

Lyle cursed again.

"Nothing. Absolutely *nothing*. She dared to touch my hand here and there and we danced. We *all* danced, not just me with her. Mel, believe me."

"You were mad at me about Ben. You were drunk and you got seduced."

"Yes. No! … Yes, I was mad and sick with anger at you, but I would never jeopardise our marriage."

"Because of the inheritance."

"Yes, because of the money my father had to slave away for for years."

Mel closed her eyes, rubbed her temples. That was the only reason. Always the stupid inheritance.

"She's just saying that to make it sell better."

"Why would she take all that to the press?"

"It's pure mockery. I told her point blank that I only want you. No one else."

"What now?" Melissa ignored her stupid heart jumping up and down at his statement.

Lyle knelt down in front of her, taking her hands in his.

"We don't let them drive us apart again. And then we'll see."

Mel looked hopefully into his eyes. She just believed everything he said, would agree to anything, just as long as he stayed with her. Had she learned nothing from her past mistakes?

~ 142 ~

Melissa hadn't quite known how to face Ally when they finally arrived at work slightly late. It turned out she didn't have to worry about that either, because she didn't come back. After some initial deliberation and mild discussion, she eventually agreed that Lyle would help out with the story writing while she and the other class teachers took care of the artistic side.

However much she resisted and would certainly never admit it in front of him, they worked well together. The days went without a hitch and the children benefited left and right from over-qualified staff members who gave their all to see them happy.

When Lyle entered the great hall at the end of the week, he saw his wife kneeling in the corner without socks or shoes, in the middle of a mess of papers and brushes, paint and glue. It looked as if a bomb had hit. She herself had paint all over her, even on her face. Several strands had come loose from her bun and she had just accidentally stepped into a water bowl.

But when she saw him coming towards her, she beamed at him. Something was moving inside him; he wasn't sure what.

He squatted in front of her and wiped some of the stains from her face.

"For a moment then, I was afraid that in desperation you would have caused this havoc yourself."

She laughed. It sounded so sincere, so real, that he laughed with her.

"It was the *best* day." she declared. And looked at the ceiling where a few drops of colour would remain forever. "Children can really be children here. No matter what it looks like afterwards. No matter how long it takes to clean up the mess. They can let off steam and experiment. And parents don't have to worry about the mess. It makes everyone happy."

Lyle agreed with her. Especially, her, by the looks of it. Her cheerfulness was infectious.

When Mel looked at him, her expression changed instantly. She leaned towards him and surprised him with an intense kiss that left no doubt what she was thinking about.

He met her halfway and with equal passion, she pushed him to the floor and sat on him before kissing him further. She was on fire, losing sense of time and space.

Lyle briefly interrupted their kiss as her hands went under his T-shirt.

"Mel, I didn't lock the door."

But she didn't care, she took his mouth again, letting her desire guide her.

"I was actually going to take you to dinner," Lyle said later, as they lay among the piles of materials for a while longer. Their hearts were still racing.

"Oh." was all she said. Her tone was less than enthusiastic.

"I mean, just you and me…. A date."

She propped herself up and looked into his face, her gaze teasing.

"Really? What are we waiting for?"

It was nice to have dinner with him *alone*, in public. It was romantic, relaxing and just perfect. She had never been able to enjoy a meal with him otherwise, always having to pretend, but this time it was *all* real.

Lyle was like a different man. He was open and warm. They talked about everything, his book, her business, his plans, her ventures.

Dinner turned into walks in the warm September sun, still soaking up the last few rays of summer. They walked hand in hand, or arm in arm. Stopping to kiss, walking on to clear their minds.

On weekends, they were inseparable. After work, they broke up early to be together. He invited her to all sorts of restaurants, even a pub. She didn't need the luxury of food, would have liked to stay at home too, but he seemed to like it.

With October, the sun was waning and their picnic in the park would probably be the last time, for a while. Melissa had packed everything that was needed. She felt a bit like the girl in Pretty Woman as she sat there laughing with him. He lay in her lap as she talked. He laughed when she was driven by her excitement. She couldn*n't* have been happier.

Melissa looked at her husband, he looked back. Without inhibition, she put her hand to his cheek and pulled him to her. It was a light kiss, yet full of emotion. Her eyes shone as she looked up. Didn't need to say anything.

Somewhere in the back of her mind she heard the clicking, felt they had been watched. And then she saw the journalist a few metres away from them.

Lyle noticed him too and surprised her by kissing her back, more passionately than expected. For all the people to see.

Mel let it happen, but deep inside she realised what had just happened here. Maybe even in the last few days. All those evenings in different restaurants, in pubs, in public. He had *planned* it all that way. Calculated it.

Her world shattered. Her heart was bleeding.

They made it to her flat before she confronted him. Her rage was almost too unbearable.

She did not wait for him to take off his jacket. Her patience had run out.

"Can this stupid show finally stop now? We're behind closed doors, aren't we?"

Lyle looked at her taken aback, not quite sure where her anger was coming from. And she really was *angry*. Her eyes were spraying fire and she was ready for a fight.

"What are you talking about?"

"*All* of these last few days had been for show." she replied, disappointed. "You've only been showing yourself outside with me, hoping someone would take a picture of the two of us. You planned it all that way."

He couldn't deny it, unfortunately. That had indeed been his plan. But he hadn't thought of it as an act.

"We have to fight this filth that Ally has been spreading. Yes, I was waiting for someone to see us."

"And I was foolish enough to assume you actually wanted to spend time with me."

He frowned at her remark.

"Didn't you enjoy our evenings then? Our nights?"

Melissa stepped further away from him, not wanting to be distracted when he held his arms out to her. She was too bitterly disappointed in his decision. Had truly believed they had become a *couple*. Obviously, they were still far from it.

"You bastard. All this to make sure I play the bloody devoted wife."

Her anger was real. Her heartbreak much greater. She should

have *known*. Why had she completely forgotten about the article on Ally? Of course, he would do *anything* to sort this out. Did she really think he'd forgotten everything around him, like she had, just because they'd spent more time together? You complete fucking idiot.

"It wasn't all that fake. Our passion is real."

She looked at him coldly. He was right. But she wanted more. *Damn it.*

"And if your plan didn't work today? Why don't you invite them here, then they can all be up close and personal with us ripping off our clothes. That's what makes our marriage real."

"We'll see how quickly they write about us. Or not." he said honestly and neutrally. He didn't necessarily want to argue with her. Maybe it would actually take him a while to convince the public again that they were a happy couple.

"That easy, huh? Let's just keep playing."

"Nothing has changed. *Why* are you so angry? What's been bothering you these past few weeks? The expensive restaurants, the theatre, the walks? What did*n't* suit you?"

Melissa felt the guilt rising inside her. Of course, it had all been nice because *he* had been by her side. They had been able to do all that because he could offer her *financial* security. After all, that was exactly what she had sold herself for.

"And all you had to do was make sure I was smiling. And nothing was easier for you than to stay close to me. Every night. Did you have to *force* yourself to do that, or did it suit you just fine?"

Her cold words cut him deeply. She didn't want to understand him. She only saw, one side of the last few weeks. It hadn't been so bad after all, making love and providing evidence that their marriage still existed. He didn't understand her anger.

"It still suits me now." he said finally. "Melissa."

She raised her hands defensively before he could get close. She knew she couldn't think straight around him. She was tired of hoping, and falling deeper every time.

"I think it's better if you go."

"Do we resume our old ways? Arguments, cold shoulders and

lies?"

"You're the one who didn't tell me what you were up to. Haven't I been doing what you want me to do all along? Even without sex? Why did you have to take advantage of our *passion*, as you so beautifully put it? I would have wanted to decide for myself how we would behave in public. Instead, you made a fool of me." Lyle stared at her in surprise. She thought he had only slept with her to keep her in a good mood. How could she think that after all these nights, days together?

"To fool you? I didn't force you to sleep with me. If I remember correctly, you are also very good at deciding what happens between us and when."

Mel felt the blush rise in her cheeks. Her lack of inhibition had gotten out of control when she was with him.

"And now I'm deciding that this show is over."

"Mel -"

"I'll be your wife if you need me in public, but otherwise I need some space."

Lyle hesitated. She'd put up another wall of protection between herself and him that he couldn't get around. He walked to the door and waited again for a moment. He looked at her.

"I really don't understand what went wrong. We were aware of the rules, weren't we? We had fun, really good sex..... Get back to me when your pride is no longer hurt."

Melissa glared blindly at the door. Her anger was still there, but only at herself. Of course, she had been aware of the damn rules. She had only lost sight of them for a moment, a brief moment. Far too long ago.

<h1 style="text-align: center;">~ 144 ~</h1>

Autumn brought many new possibilities and colours. The children loved the new utensils that Mel brought them. They discovered again, the different shades in leaves and chestnuts, acorns and berries.

She loved her work here. She loved that she could spend all day here and not think or want to think about anything else for one second. She was completely absorbed here. In the evenings she had started to paint and draw herself again. She had been sent a few offers to illustrate novels and she had her hands full.

Which was just as well. Lyle complied with her demands and stayed away. To be precise, he was no longer in the office next door. Was no longer in the building. Once again, he seemed to be able to go days without contacting her.

That's what you wanted! screamed a voice inside her. She was so torn, and so confused. What do you want if you don't like him staying away from you?

Sex or love, you can't have both. Make up your bloody mind.

Melissa pushed her wild thoughts far away again, and concentrated on her sketch. It had been dark outside for a long time when she stood in front of her canvas and put her ideas for the new book on paper. Again and again, she had to start over because her thoughts wanted to run away, or she accidentally drew Lyle and not the character from the book. Or she got lost in the picture and it screamed kitsch novel.

She crumpled the page again and threw it to the floor.

Mel heard his footsteps, smelled his aftershave before she saw him in her office. She was relieved that it had only taken a week before he realised, he still wanted her by his side, and in his bed.

When she turned back to him, she froze.

His long coat hung open, his shirt underneath a total mess, he wore no tie. His hair was wild, wilder than usual. Worst of all, though, was his gaze. Ice cold. Bitter. Off-Dismissive.

Lyle held a newspaper in his hand. Mel immediately realised the cause of his visit and assumed that the story about their marriage had probably not been interpreted correctly after all and that his plan had backfired.

"Have you fallen in love with me?"

Mel was struck by his question like lightning. Her heart stopped; she didn't move a muscle. She couldn't answer, didn't know how. *Shit.*

He came up to her and held the front of the newspaper up to her face. It was a perfect picture of them together, in the park. Their heads close together, smiles on their faces. And Mel's beaming eyes.

Mel saw the title and everything inside her tightened.

If that isn't true love, what is?

She swallowed dryly. She lifted her gaze determinedly and met his. It became clear to her that he believed the photo and the headline. It was obvious, after all. Any blind person could recognise the way she looked at him. This had not been an act. This was one hundred percent real.

"Do you love me?" he repeated his question, with an immense insistence that sent shivers down her spine. Something was going wrong here. This wasn't how a declaration of love turned out in a book. As soon as he knew she loved him, he would confess his undying love to her. What was going on *here*?

She put down her pencils, put away the newspaper and straightened up. Everything was over. No more acting, no more lies.

"Yes." she answered honestly and then much more forcefully. She ignored how he literally flinched at her words and moved miles away from her. Not at all like in her dreams. This was definitely *not* how she had imagined this moment a thousand times before. She had not rehearsed this scenario even once. "Yes, I love you... God knows why."

Lyle paced back and forth, *stressed!* He was unhappy that she had feelings for him, but she hadn't expected such a bitterly huge disappointment from him. It broke her heart *twice*; he didn't love her back and he hated the thought of her doing so.
He couldn't look at her, seemed to be struggling with himself.
"The whole point of this marriage was for us not to have feelings for each other. Why did you have to put all that at risk?"
"Believe me, I didn't set out to do that. And I'm trying to deal with it myself."
"Melissa, what the hell were you playing at?"
"I've been right in front of you. Every day, every night. And it took a newspaper to show you? A fucking blurry picture of us together?"
He was completely beside himself, had really convinced himself that there was *nothing* more.
She couldn't believe they were both arguing about her *loving* him. This was supposed to be the most beautiful feeling ever. It was supposed to free them both and give them a chance to be happy with each other. Instead, it drove them so far apart that Mel couldn't reach him.
"The rules were set out clear as!" he repeated in exasperation. "There was no mention of love."
"As if I didn't know that." she countered coldly. "But for sex, this marriage was good enough. Oh yes, and children would have fitted in too."
She crossed her arms in annoyance. She didn't want to have to justify herself, had enough to cope with herself that *she* hadn't prevented it. She knew how everything ended, after all.
"We had an agreement."
"It can stay in place."
"No."
"Why not?"
"Is it because of the last few months? I should have kept more to myself. Like I did in the house. I should have stayed out of your way more."
Melissa looked at him astonished as he really blamed himself

for her falling for him. He paced back and forth impatiently, looking confused and almost desperate. Had he no idea how love worked?

"Is that why you were so unapproachable? All those arguments, the weeks spent alone, just so I wouldn't fall for you?" She finally understood why they could never find each other. No matter how hot the nights, the days were always freezing cold. He had been trying to stop her from liking him. Well, that had *bloody* backfired. "Tough luck, I fell head over heels in love with you the moment I first walked down the stairs in your house."

"That was years ago!"

"Yes .... years ago." she replied as unimpressed as he had just been. It had taken her a long time to come to terms with it herself.

Lyle fell silent, running a tired, weary hand through his hair. For days he had lingered over this article, over this *picture*. He had thought back and forth about what it would mean for him and for this marriage. He saw no other way out, no solution, no hope.

He stopped instantly and his eyes were cool and distant. No longer hasty, or wild. When he spoke, his words were clear. He had made a decision for them both, there was no way back.

"I will give you your freedom back.... I will consent to the divorce - in nine months or a year at the latest."

She froze on the spot. *No.*

"I need that time for legal reasons, be patient for that time ... still play along. By then I have managed to ask one of my trusted sponsors to invest in your business so that it can continue and be financially secure. He will divest himself of my business so you can be sure it is *your* company and has nothing to do with McClory."

Melissa had been holding her breath. Whatever she had expected, this had not been it. Her freedom? The divorce? After all this time, this struggle? She felt the despair rising inside her, the grief, the fear of being without him, the panic that he could leave at any moment and she would never see him again. He had considered all the details and come up with solutions. He made sure how he could save her children without being in the least bit connected to her anymore. What she had always wanted. Completely and utterly independent of *him*.

"You give up your entire inheritance, just like that. Your father's hard-earned money? Just because I *love* you?"

"Unlove me." he demanded helplessly.

But they both knew it was far too late for that. Everything was so bleak at that moment. Their hearts empty, their hopes gone as if they had vanished into thin air.

"Don't *you* love *me*?" She held her breath. She realised with a heavy heart that she wanted nothing more than for him to want her by his side. At least for a few more weeks, days - even hours, just so she could show him that her love didn't have to be an obstacle. They had made it thus far. Couldn't he pretend that this photo had never appeared?

Lyle's gaze was pained. He looked her straight in the eye. He wasn't angry, wasn't confused anymore. No, he had resigned himself to the fact that this was the end of ... *her*.

"I'll send you the papers when it's all arranged." He hesitated. "I can't give you any more."

Mel wanted to object. In her mind she was close to begging. What had he done to her? She thought of approaching him and kissing him and ... forcing her way to his love? How much further was she supposed to sink?

It was useless, her love was not reciprocated. He had never promised her anything else, they had agreed on that. Nothing, absolutely *nothing* more. So why did she feel so, *so* empty? So alone and ... disappointed?

Everything in her, every single fibre wanted to stop him. Everything in her cried out, resisting his plans, his neutral demeanour. But she had no excuse to stop him, nothing more to add. Everything that needed to be said had been said. He knew of her love, was averse to it. He had made the decision; he had thought carefully about what was good for her. Her business could remain. Now it was just a matter of waiting for him to sort out everything financially and legally before they could sign the divorce papers.

Lyle looked at his wife's face one last time, wanting to remember it.

Melissa didn't move an inch from the spot.

And let him go.

~ EPILOG ~

The last, warm rays of the sun. Winter, spring, summer - her spirits had lifted from month to month. Now with autumn came dark clouds, rain, cold. The nights became longer again. Much, much too long. But *not* today. Today the sun was shining for her again, helping her through the long-awaited day.

Melissa lifted her face to the sun after making the final preparations for her big day. She had organised her own children's party for today during the autumn holidays. After weeks of planning and arranging, she had managed to give her little artists a party they would never forget. All sorts of illustrators with the most diverse, iconic styles were invited to show children free painting techniques and maybe even try them out themselves. Several successful children's authors were there to read their own stories as well as those published monthly. It meant everything for their children to see their own books and illustrations and for others to appreciate them.

Mel looked contentedly at the field and the various event tents. The weather was kind to her, it was almost the end of October. She felt the warmer air warming her senses too.

Today would be a good day, for sure.

A deep stab went through her heart and she stopped her thoughts instantly. She knew exactly where they would lead her and today was not the day. Tomorrow neither. This grief, this pain had to come to an end, it had been almost a year. Every day she fought this emptiness, found distraction in her work, but no real happiness. She missed *him* so much.

If you can get through today, you've made it. Today was the deadline, today was the last day of her contract. As of tomorrow, she had a new sponsor for her company. It was only a few more hours and then she was independent.

Then they were divorced.

Stop it, she scolded herself, before feeling sorry for herself again. You can do that later, when you're alone. Now you belong to the children.

It was an exhausting day, the constant smiling, the listening, the cheering up, the drawing and the reading, but it was all worth every second. She could see it in their faces, in their eyes. They were all beaming, taking with them the best memories and their achievements of a day.

Deeply satisfied, but also absolutely exhausted, they set about clearing away. She had hired several helpers, and her loyal staff was firmly on the case.

Joshua came over to her and took some of the things she wanted to put on the tables. He smiled at her and continued to work busily. He deserved the biggest bonus she could afford, she thought in retrospect. They had both worked day and night to make this day perfect.

Mel laughed into his eyes. They were such a great team, even now after the work was done, he didn't show any signs of tiredness or rush to get away. He worked briskly alongside her.

"You were great." he said sincerely, with a loving tone. Mel's heart warmed.

Then he lowered his head and continued undisturbed, his voice this time calm and firm. "*He* is standing right behind us."

Mel's breath caught only fleetingly as his words entered her mind. Josh watched her regain her composure within seconds and continue in her work as if everything was normal. As it had been for almost a year. He admired this woman. How could she suffer so much from a broken heart and yet seem so strong? She was one of a kind. If he wasn't already marrying his best friend next month, she was the woman who could change his mind.

"Maybe you should still help with the tents..." she suggested. She didn't know what to expect from her reunion with her *husband*. In any case, she didn't want any spectators. Her stomach tightened brutally, which annoyed her and she immediately ignored her nerves.

"Shall I give you a kiss .... for show?"

Mel laughed heartily at his remark. He had meant it, too. Wanted to somehow help her get through the next few minutes. She was immensely grateful to him for that.

She straightened up from her work.

"That won't be necessary." She smiled at him one last time before turning to her husband.

All these months she had convinced herself that her feelings for Lyle had been nothing more than infatuation from the ground up. He didn't mean that much to her. She was over him. All that had ever connected them had been pure lust. Nothing more. He was cold as ice and arrogant, could never admit when he was wrong. He was a workaholic, like her actually, and he never allowed time for her. She couldn't remember at all why she *should* love him. It was all in her head. Finally, today she could prove to herself what she had been telling herself. She was over him. Absolutely and totally.

Then she saw him.

You idiot. There's no way you're over him. Never ever. *Shit.*

He was standing just a few steps away from her, in his smart suit, his perfectly tied tie. His hair cropped short but still wild. His blue eyes *fixed* on her.

She was speechless. He had managed to have that effect on her many times before, just with his presence. Her heart pounded in her throat. Her knees weak.

How could he do this to her over and over again? Even after all this time? And today, even *more* so.

Today! They were a few hours away from their divorce and here he was. With the papers in his hand.

She was not sure why he had come himself. He could have sent the papers. She wouldn't have sent them before the deadline. His presence irritated her instantly. Why did he have to show up here? Why the hell hadn't he stayed away? All sorts of emotions were swirling around inside her. She did not know how to face him. Forgot how to talk all of a sudden. Was totally dissatisfied with herself.

Lyle hesitated himself. What had he expected? What had he wanted to say? What was he thinking right now, seeing her standing here in front of him, in her jeans and sweatshirt, full of paint stains and glue? Her hair wild, glitter on her cheeks.

She would probably never know.

"Mrs McClory, what a success!" A man in his mid-fifties came walking quickly towards her, hand stretched out and a broad smile on his lips. Then he saw Lyle and his face showed even greater joy. "Ah, Lyle! That's handy that you're right here too."

Melissa's nerves ran out and she couldn't help a relieved smirk at this interruption. She lowered her gaze for a moment to hide her reaction. Lyle barely noticed it before he greeted Victor Thompson.

His voice cut deep into her soul. Yes, by no means. She was by no means over him.

"Victor, good to see you here too, supporting the company of my ... wife."

Mel quietly took a deep breath and exhaled.

"Haven't you forgotten something?" she said cautiously.

Lyle held her gaze. He hadn't forgotten *anything*. Not an hour, not a minute. He still held the envelope tightly in his hand.

"I mean, my incredibly talented wife." He raised an eyebrow slightly raised. Challenge accepted.

Victor laughed at his statement, seeming oblivious to the heightened mood between them.

"Utterly talented. I'm looking forward to it now, to our collaboration. You didn't promise too much." he agreed frankly. "There are one or two little things I wanted to discuss with you both. All the better to find you together, how about dinner later? Iron out the last details and then we can sign all our papers."

Now she didn't feel like smirking. Mel tensed inwardly at his suggestion. Signing the paper was one thing, spending another evening by Lyle's side was another. She was still his *wife*, had to

pretend to be. Could she still do that? Did she still *want* to?
Lyle met her uneasy gaze. He sensed her resistance, knew exactly what was going on inside her right now.
"I have an early flight and Melissa -"
"I won't keep you long. That will leave you the rest of the night to say goodbye." Victor laughed himself at his insinuation and with that he went on his way. It was a done deal; if she wanted him as a lucrative sponsor, she would have to perform as Lyle's wife again tonight.
"He's been dragging this out for months - "
"No problem." she interrupted him coldly and set about cleaning up further.
"He's the best sponsor for your children ... " he tried to defend himself again. He was at a loss for the right words. He saw her moving away from him. He followed her.
"You're celebrating great success, Melissa. You've come a long way." he said sincerely, nodding at the many tents and eager workers.
She stared at him.
"You mean I didn't perish after you fled my *love*." she replied, in a neutral tone. "Love is not a handicap."
Lyle fell silent as if struck.
Mel said goodbye to a couple of writers, and began to help her helpers dismantle and pack everything away. She used as much time as possible to give her instructions.
Lyle gave up.
"I can see I'm in the way here." he said coldly.
Melissa carried a few boxes from the tents to the van. Lyle still at her heels.
She had to work hard not to welcome him with open arms and heart. She couldn't start all that fuss again. She still wasn't over their breakup. She couldn't open up all those wounds again.
She was getting angrier inside that he had dared to come here. Didn't he realise what this would do to her? Was he going to relish in her misery?
"Why didn't you send the papers?"

He looked down at the envelope suddenly, as if he had completely forgotten it was still in his hand.

"I wanted to make sure they'd arrive on time."

"The deadline is midnight tonight. You're not a minute early." she said coldly, looking blatantly at her watch. "Leave them here and I'll sign them first thing in the morning."

She held her hand out to him, impatient and bitter. She just wanted to get it over with now. She had to get away from him, didn't want to deal with it, here in public. She couldn't break down in front of everyone when she saw his signature on the divorce papers. She had to prepare herself physically and mentally. The last few months hadn't been enough for her to accept. A lifetime wasn't going to be enough.

But Lyle did not hand her the envelope, instead he took her hand.

She shuddered at his touch. As if burned, she withdrew it from him and stared warningly into his face.

"Don't do that." She felt her body on the brink of falling. She was so close to showing him her true feelings, the inner turmoil that nearly broke her and would drive her into his arms. "A contract is a contract."

Lyle didn't respond to her cold words. He had felt the shock as much as she had. She was nowhere near as neutral to him as she pretended to be. And neither was he.

"Yes, the contract stands. My promise too." he confirmed quietly. "I think we should wait until after dinner before we sign the papers."

"No. We're just going round in circles." She stopped herself in her words before she gave too much away.

"It will make the time go by faster."

Mel closed her eyes for a moment. Maybe he was right, time would pass faster if she didn't have to sit at home alone and wait for every second to tick by. But back in a restaurant with him as his wife? Did that help or did it just make everything that much more unbearable?

"Fine. For an hour."

Lyle nodded.

"I'll pick you up." He hesitated when she said nothing. "Is it still the same address?" he finally asked.

Melissa looked at his face in disbelief. Then she picked up a few more boxes.

"Yes. *Nothing* ... has changed."

And with that she left him standing there.

~ 146 ~

Lyle picked her up from her flat on time. Nothing *had* changed, everything was the same as it had been a year ago. As if he had never been away. But he had been, and would be forever. Tonight was the last evening she would spend with him. The last five hours of their marriage had begun. After these four turbulent years, which they had spent more often apart than together, they were finally drawing a line under it. It was about time. There was no other solution. They were only making each other unhappy. Neither of them could go on living their lives like this.

Lyle looked at her silently as she came down the stairs in her long evening dress. She was a gorgeous woman, his *wife*. At least until midnight. His gaze was infinitely intense. She got goose bumps when she looked into his eyes. Her heart contracted painfully. She would have liked to turn back and flee to her safe, lonely flat.

He hesitated only a moment, but then he could not help but follow his emotions. He kissed her gently on the cheek and slowly pulled away.

Her gaze closed off; her eyes darkened.

"Please don't." A spark stood in her eyes. This tenderness was far too much for her to bear. He had so much power over her. It was destructively attracting. She took another step back, up the step. Panic rose in his eyes, instantly regretting what he had done.

"It's not a good idea. I can't come with you."

"I'm sorry. That wasn't fair." he said immediately, holding up his hands. His voice was pleading. "I'm keeping my distance. Please

…. join me."

Melissa hesitated for a long while. Wrestling with herself, with her heart that bled silently, with her head that screamed at her not to make the *same* mistake again. She was torn.

Finally, she took a deep breath and followed him to his car. It was business after all. She had to play his wife one more time to finally lock this sponsor into a contract. For months he had dragged his feet to sign himself over to her company. A large amount of commitment and money was at stake, she understood his hesitation. But it was nerve wracking nonetheless.

The drive to the restaurant seemed to take ages. They were silent the whole time. Admittedly, she was grateful that she had more time to concentrate on herself than sitting at a table with him. She thought about all the things she could talk about without really talking about herself. She remembered what she should definitely not do: touch him however innocently, smell him especially when he took off his jacket, or look him in the eyes, because then she would lose herself in them. All she had to do was stick to those rules and the evening would be over in a flash. She could stick to rules, couldn't she?

Mmmmh, last time she had fallen hopelessly in love.

When they arrived, she got out immediately before he got the idea to hold the door for her and stand in front of her. She looked at the large restaurant in front of her. They were well practised at pretending to be a couple, why did it have to be as difficult for her today as it had been the first time? She felt uncomfortable. Fortunately, all those odd rules still existed about not giving each other affection in public. She had never been *more* grateful. Victor was already sitting at the table and saw the couple arrive from a distance. He greeted them both warmly and immediately got down to business.

Mel was relieved because at least she could keep up with the conversation. It was about her dream, her business and her excitement and energy showed in her expectations and ideas. Victor nodded with satisfaction and added a few ideas here and there.

Lyle tried to keep the conversation neutral and talked about his new book and release date. She talked about her business and the many small events that kept her going and gave her the strength to get up every day. Of course, she had not expressed herself in this way. She had not forgotten how to talk calmly and sincerely about her work, her goals and new projects. It felt good. Lyle seemed genuinely interested in hearing about what she had done. He let them talk and took it all in quietly and calmly. He looked proud of her.

They both poked at their food, unable to discuss what was really on their minds.

"And what do I hear from you, projects in America?"

Lyle cleared his throat and shifted a little in his seat. Mel looked at him. All at once she felt awful. She was already cut out of his life; had had no idea he was going to America and what projects? Why *should* she know anything about that either? When should he have told her about it?

"Starting tomorrow, we want to work on bringing out another children's series out there."

She swallowed dryly. Tomorrow already? Who was his new illustrator? Was she also fully cut out of his stories from now on? She felt sick to her stomach. Her stomach twisted bitterly. She fought against this endless *emptiness* that was spreading through her. She took a sip of her water. She needed distraction. She took a deep breath and instantly regretted it. His aftershave smelled so *good*. Melissa, remember your own rules!

"I must admit, the way you two conduct your marriage only gives us mere mortals hope. Your long-distance relationship is always in the papers. You've worked out how it is done."

Victor took a big gulp of his wine and smiled at them both. Lyle put his hand on hers, twirling her wedding ring with his thumb. Why hadn't she taken that ring off long ago? It did her no good to wear it. It only reminded her, day in and day out, that Lyle was *gone*. He had already seen her ring in the field. It had sparkled at him in the bright sunlight, had given him an odd feeling.

"It's going to be hard to get used to it to start with." He said eva-

sively, looking lovingly at Mel. His touch burned her skin, made her body ache deeply, sensually. Her desire for him was unbearable. She had already broken two of her self-set rules. *Damn.*
She just smiled at him.
Victor excused himself for a moment to go to the bathroom. Immediately she withdrew her hand and visibly moved a little away from him.
"He talks a lot." said Lyle quietly, trying to distract her. He could sense her tenseness. "The contracts are signed. He's agreed to everything and more. Nothing stands in the way of your success."
Melissa played with the glass in her hand. Her company was now her everything. As it had been for so long. She was looking forward to achieving everything she could imagine. Only who would she be able to tell about it?
"I still find these evenings -"
She stopped abruptly in her sentence and became aware of her thoughts. She'd had enough lying to herself.
Lyle's eyebrows drew together. Why wasn't she continuing to talk?
"Melissa?"
She looked up and into his eyes. His beautiful blue eyes. Even if he could never *love* her, that blue was unforgettable and would always touch her deeply. She held his gaze. Rule number three had been broken. She was lost.
"Unbearable." she finished her sentence. And saw that he knew exactly why she had hesitated.
He didn't answer, but they both felt the unspoken feelings hanging in the air, felt the electricity coming from them both. Just one little spark and they would burn themselves to the soul. Again. Or still?
Victor came back to the table and saw exactly the same thing. He smirked slightly to himself. As he had said, there was a lot of envy where their relationship was concerned.
They managed to finish the evening and Lyle offered Victor a ride to his house. Less time alone in the car, all the better.

The last few minutes to her flat felt like years. Melissa glanced unnoticed at her watch and realised it was still three and a half hours until midnight.

She stopped in front of the stairs to say goodbye to him. He kept a good distance from her, as she had asked him to. He was so *damn* good at sticking to rules. The stupid envelope in his hand.

"What time is your flight?"

Lyle didn't bother to look at his watch. He didn't take his eyes off her. She looked tired. Sad?

"In the morning."

Melissa was silent. Torn with what she wanted to do, should do, had to do. Couldn't he make the start? Go, stay, kiss her, anything?

"The papers - "

Not that, she thought desperately, taking a step towards him.

"Not yet." she whispered defensively and decisively. She was close enough in front of him now that he, too, inhaled her scent. Tantalisingly sweet. He fought with himself not to brush the unruly strands of hair from her face.

"If I touch you now, I don't know if I can stop." He admitted breathlessly. His throat so dry. His whole body vibrating.

Melissa decided for them both.

"Don't...."

They met at the same moment, receiving the kiss with a passion that made her giddy. Mel reached for his arms to keep her footing, then put her arms around his neck to pull him close. His kiss was demanding, so stunningly sensual. She met him with equal lust, leaving nothing hidden. Lyle struggled for his sanity, trying to restrain himself but it was no use. He had to feel her, had to touch her - everywhere. He kissed her neck and something broke inside as he took in the long-awaited little noises she made.

Melissa trembled all over and stepped away from him for a moment. His gaze dark, slightly confused. She grabbed his hand and pulled him with her to the front door. He followed her without hesitation, gently stroking her hair from her neck and kissing her neck as she dealt with the key. Then they came to her front door and again they had to hold back for a moment.

Finally, the door fell into the lock and they were alone and inseparable. They didn't need to say another word, found their way into her bedroom, dropping their clothes where they were. Melissa arched towards him with everything she had.

~ 147 ~

Melissa opened her eyes as Lyle sat up. He sat still at the side of her bed. He did not move. Did he regret it?

"Lyle?"

He didn't look at her, just shook his head slightly.

"Mel, I couldn't..., I... I should have had more restraint."

She sat up abruptly.

"Stop it." she said forcefully and clearly. She stood up to make her answer more explicit. "You don't have to feel bad. I'm not the same person I was four years ago. You didn't overwhelm me. Not at all." she said coolly. "I probably wanted it a lot more than you did."

With that, she fled to the bathroom. She needed a moment alone. Her whole body was still quivering. She had never been one for sex in the past, but with Lyle it was a whole new experience. She could never get enough of him, and just now it had been like an uncontrollable explosion. It had hit her totally unexpectedly. How could she feel so intensely for one person? This desire, this pure lust seemed to have only grown in his absence. Never, ever had she imagined such a reunion. And she wanted more. Didn't want to let him *go*.

When Mel came back into the bedroom, he was no longer on the bed, his clothes no longer on the floor. She hastily pulled on a pair of jeans and blouse and sought him out. He wasn't going to leave already, was he?

She found him in the living room by the door, envelope in hand. Her heart sank. She felt a chill.

"You're just going to make a run for it?" Her head and mind were in turmoil. Just a moment ago they had loved each other, given each other everything possible and now this! She felt betrayed and ...

And she got *angry*. Hot tears came to her eyes, which only made her *angrier*!

"Oh Mel, you see, this is exactly what I didn't want. Now you're crying because of me." He looked shaken and annoyed. A dichotomy of emotions on his face. "I've never seen you cry before."

"I'm not crying, you idiot! That's anger." She responded icily and had instantly regained her composure. "I swore years ago I would never cry again. Not even because of you.... Especially not because of you."

Lyle's eyebrows drew together and he returned her cold front just as easily as so many times before. Nothing had changed in this regard.

He recognised her more like that. He was relieved.

"The divorce stands."

"Fine, as long as you tell me why you won't give us a chance." she challenged him. Her heart ached. The last thing she wanted to do right now was talk about it or even think about it. But it didn't help. There were only two hours to go and then he was *out* of her life. She had to hear why. Otherwise, she would spend the rest of her life fantasising about it.... and *hope*.

"No. It doesn't matter. Our contract is up."

"Well, at least you stuck to the rules to the bitter end. *Bravo*!"

"I wanted to give you everything. Financial security, a stable marriage. You seemed content with that." Lyle suddenly seemed tired and at the end of his strength to argue back.

Mel nodded slightly. It had been enough for her then, too.

"I was. I really wanted to abide by your rules. I was doing what you expected me to do... in public at least."

Lyle looked straight at her. That was *exactly* the problem.

"And you *still* would." he added to her statement. "I don't want you to lose your happiness and your passion. I don't want you to tie yourself to me and one day think how unhappy you've been. All this time. That's why I'm letting you go."

Mel felt this conversation going only one way. The divorce was imminent and she did*n't* want it. Had never really wanted it. Her life without him was bleak. She had everything she wanted and valued it too. But it would only ever be *almost* complete. She would never be *whole* without him.

Her last chance was now. She couldn't do more than lose him. Wasn't it worth a try?

She approached him impatiently and forced him to look at her and not avoid her. Where she got this courage from, she did not know.

"But don't you see that you are my happiness? That you hold my passion in your hands? No matter how much I fight it, *you* are the reason I am either whole or always feel this emptiness. You're the last piece I need in my life."

Lyle lowered his gaze, unable to look her in the eye, not wanting to hear how much she loved him. He was so worried that he couldn't give her what she deserved. And she deserved *everything*. Was he really ready to put away all his past failures and hope that he would never disappoint her?

"It's better if we separate." he repeated again, unmoved by her words, and by her annoyed look. "Before I hurt you."

"You're hurting me by not giving us a chance."

Melissa took new courage.

"Don't you love me?" she asked urgently. Her heart pounded so loudly he had to hear it. She could hear the blood rushing through her veins in her ears. She felt hopeful. It was not the first time she had asked him that. But today it seemed to her that maybe his answer would be *different*. "Look me in the eye and tell me you feel nothing for me but lust and desire?"

He hesitated at least; she would find support in that later. He looked her straight in the eye, just as she had demanded. That would *break* her later.

"Nothing else, Mel.... no."

Mel remained silent. All her hopes shattered. Her heart lay in shards.

"I can't make you happy." he continued again. He was torn. His fear of hurting her was unbearable. But the thought of letting her go seemed much *more* unbearable. Could he really live another day without her? Did he still want to?

Melissa gathered her strength and stepped as close to him as she could. She grabbed his hand and placed it on her heart.

"Feel for yourself how much *you* move me. Deep inside."

She pressed her lips tightly to his, momentarily very afraid of whether he would reject her. But after a split second, he opened to her kiss and returned her desire, with an intensity that left her weak.

Lyle felt her heart beat stronger, harder and galloping under his hand.

He wanted to be so close to her, but couldn't lose his composure...not again. He just knew so well what she was doing to him and how this would end. Just for one more brief moment, really enjoying this passion. It felt perfect.

Because it was *meant to be*, it cried out inside him.

But it was Mel herself who stopped for a moment. Enough to put a few inches between them. Enough to get some air.

"I want you by my side. I want to tell you at night what we've achieved. I want to see the pride in your eyes when we win awards. I want to go with you to your stiff events, and see the envy on all the women's faces that *I* am by your side.... I want you beside me, in my bed."

She kissed him again, passionately and without doubt. He recognised her desire and brought the same lust towards her. She tasted so sweet, so tempting. He couldn't resist her, wanted her as much as she wanted him. Oh, she was driving him crazy.

No, the other way around. She made him understand.

"Melissa, wait."

Breathless, he let go of her and looked deep into her eyes. He had to be able to see her love, couldn't ignore it anymore. She looked stunning. Her eyes so dark from the passion that connected them so much. Her cheeks slightly flushed from the heat that had risen in them both. How had he stayed away from her for so long? How had he been able to push her away?

Lyle tried to sort out his thoughts and took some steps from her.

He had forgotten for a moment why they couldn't be together.

"I was married before."

Melissa stared at him in disbelief. The desire inside her momentarily lost as she tried to make sense of what he was trying to tell her.

Another marriage, another woman.

He loved *someone else*.

Still did.

She took several steps away from him. Took a moment to digest his words, to take in. So he *really* didn't love her. Didn't actually want to give them a chance because he couldn't. His heart was already taken.

What now? She felt a slight panic rise in her. She was trembling. She felt sick. So incredibly sick.

Lyle ran a tired hand over his face, and when he looked at her again, she saw pain and regret. Just unhappiness in his eyes. She didn't want to see that sadness anymore, was ready to sign the divorce papers immediately. She could not compete with another woman.

"And you love her ... still." she finished his statement for him.

"Probably, yes." He didn't see Mel flinch slightly at his answer. He saw nothing in front of him but an image of a young woman. "Jasmine."

Mel brought all her strength and confidence to stand strong and unmoved opposite him. When all she wanted to do was ... cry. For so long she had resisted such weak emotions, but the disappointment, the sadness, the realisation of never being able to win him over brought her to her knees.

She stood still, straight and proud. And waited. He did not see her. Was busy with his own painful memories.

Lyle was the first to move and he went to his jacket, which he had thrown on the kitchen counter, hurriedly before.... Her heart kept breaking.

He pulled a small box from his jacket pocket. Somewhat ponderously, he opened it and took out the tie clip.

Melissa was completely confused when she recognised her gift from four years ago. The one that had gone so wrong. She had long since put those memories out of her mind. She didn't need to mention her failures again. And yet it all seemed like yesterday to her. Her time with Lyle. And now it was coming to an end. He twisted the tie clip back and forth in his fingers, stroked the engraving meaningfully. *Salerno.*

"My name is actually Lyle Salerno. My mother's maiden name." he said as if to himself with a contemptuous short laugh, his gaze fixed on the clip. But his hands were shaking as he packed it away again. "Your gift brought me back to reality and I didn't want to. Wanted to ignore it as much as I could. You made a mess of everything. Unintentionally, yet from the ground up."

Melissa was silent. She was freezing, she could barely breathe.

She couldn't understand everything at once. Her present had been a complete misstep, even though it was actually his real name? How did something like that happen? She didn't dare ask, waiting for him to answer voluntarily.

Lyle remained silent for a long time. After a while he walked towards her sofa and sat down resignedly. He had never talked about it to anyone, except people who had been in his life at the time. He didn't want to dig in those wounds. But he wanted even less for Melissa to misunderstand him. It all had to end today.

"I just couldn't bear to hear the name anymore, changed it to erase everything that had happened in my past from my life.... To cut her out of my life." he began quietly, his gaze lowered, unmoving on his hands. He spoke as if to himself and to her, his *first* wife. He saw a wedding ring that had not been there for a long time.

She sensed the tension in him, the unease and rush of emotion.

"I haven't been to see her for fifteen years.... To see my wife's *grave.*"

An ice-cold shiver came over her at his words. Word by word his story penetrated her consciousness. Word for word she saw the pain he was still struggling with. She took a seat next to him on the sofa. Enough distance between them.

Melissa stared at the man in disbelief, thinking of the name, the meaning. She felt cold. She was deeply shaken and tried to understand what he was telling her here. Her mind overflowed with her theories and answers to countless questions about his past.

"I don't want pity." he spoke immediately when he met her gaze. He shook his head. "I'm telling you this now so you know what it means to be with me and why I *don't* want your love."

She looked him straight in the face. She was really confused. Whatever she had imagined because of his past, it had not been a *wife*. Especially not a dead wife. If he had told her about his best friend Verona now, yes, everything would have been clear to her. Instead, they sat here and he used Jasmine to deny himself her love.

Mel heard the tremor in his voice and instinctively took his hand. With the other, she turned his head towards her. No matter how sad she herself was, she couldn't take the sadness in his face. It only broke her heart more. Where was his cold demeanour, his protective wall that he usually had around him?

"You don't have to talk about it if you don't want to ... can't...."

Lyle leaned his forehead against hers. He closed his eyes and took a deep breath in and out. Then he let go of her and slid a little away.

"I want you to at least know the truth before we end this marriage." he said urgently, his hands clenching, his face contorted in pain.

Melissa nodded slightly, feeling the urge to want to do something. She went into the kitchen to give him a moment alone. She had felt him struggling with himself, not knowing what to do. But at least here today he was mentally with his wife.

The darkness outside and the quaint silence made her nervous, but she waited patiently. For a few moments she forgot her own worries and thoughts and tried not to let her imagination run wild about what he might have to tell her. This time he would tell her *himself*, perhaps too late.

She placed two glasses on the table in front of her.

Melissa was nervous, anxious and curious about what he was

going to tell her. He had never been forthcoming about his past. Had always been quite dismissive if she even mentioned it. Everyone knew about it, but not her. Now she wanted to know the truth, as shocking and sad as it might be.

"Jasmine Salerno." she said carefully, trying her hand at the subject again.

Lyle didn't avoid her gaze, wanting to tell her everything.

"We got married so young. She had only been 18 and I was 21. We hadn't even really got to know each other yet. But it seemed like the right decision. We were totally in love too." He remembered the initial time, which had been so carefree and so free. A wistful smile played on his lips; his eyes warm. "My father had his reservations, so did her parents, and we felt it. I was fresh out of university, no job, nothing. Jasmine had just finished school. We had no support, nothing. And we were so stubborn, so stupid. So in love."

He shook his head almost ruefully as he remembered their life together then. Couldn't understand at all now what had made them be so reluctant to take advice and so naive.

"We lived in a tiny little flat, with just a bed and some furniture. It didn't seem all that important to find work, save money or buy food. We lived in our selective poverty for months."

Melissa listened to him in silence, learning a whole new side to him.

"I finally came to my senses and wanted to get us out of this hole, out of this hell. And I found work for all sorts of magazines. I was good at writing short stories and gradually spent more time at work than I did with her."

Lyle ran a weary hand through his hair. Those times had been the darkest times in his life. He had done everything he could to forget them, to never mention them. But today he wanted Mel to hear about it. That she knew everything.

"I didn't want to be home anymore. Jasmine was always so sad and unhappy. No matter what I achieved, no matter how much money I made, she was ... moody and unapproachable." He shook his head slightly. Still felt her distaste for him. "I met

Verona."

Mel sat up involuntarily. This woman had always been a thorn in her eye. So had she been right after all? Did she want to have been right?

"Verona was a bit older than me, had married just as young. She seemed to regret it very much. She kept telling me how much she wanted a divorce and didn't want to be with Richard at all anymore. And I told her about Jasmine and her moods. We spent a lot of time together. It was obvious what she wanted. I know she still hasn't forgiven herself for that even today."

He put his hand over his mouth. Silent for a long moment to catch himself before he could finish the story.

"You and Verona ..." Mel asked hesitantly, feeling the pressure in her heart as if she had been his wife Jasmine. A fist grabbed her heart and squeezed. She held her breath, not sure she could bear the truth.

"No, Mel. I didn't let myself be seduced. Not then, not now." His eyes showed guilt despite all that, but she believed him. Wanted to believe him, why would he tell her all this and lie about it.

"I knew what Verona wanted. I also knew the appearance of our friendship. But I had more important things on my mind. I almost worked myself to death so that we lacked nothing. We finally had a better, expensive accommodation, Jasmine didn't have to go to work...."

Lyle stopped to drink some of the water. He couldn't look Mel in the eye, he clenched his hands together until his knuckles stood out white.

"The days alone in our expensive flat got worse and worse for Jasmine. Many days I came back in the evening and she had not left her bed. Other days I found her standing at the window ... naked, because she couldn't remember where her clothes were. Sometimes she smiled, most of the time she looked at me crossly, showing no pleasure in seeing me. I had no understanding, was driven by this compulsion to work and earn more, more money for us."

He shook his head as if to himself. As if scolding himself, over and over again.

"For her Christmas present, I had bought her a precious necklace. I wanted to surprise her with it and prove to her that I did everything for *her*.... On Christmas Eve, I had just wanted to catch up with something, had been just a little late so that we could go to church together. I was late. I found her in the bathroom. Alone, way too late."

Melissa held her breath. She felt his pain and shock. At that moment, he must have blamed himself.

"Lyle..." Her voice soft and soothing. "Christmas... now I understand..."

"Richard had called her. Filling her head with *his* ideas what was going on between his wife and myself. Jasmine thought we were having an affair and I didn't contradict her. Could never tell her I had never cheated on her. She took her own life because of me. She loved me and I destroyed her."

Mel shook her head decisively and put her hand on his cheek. She waited until he looked at her. The pain so deep in his eyes she flinched herself.

"Lyle, you alone couldn't have helped her." she said softly. "Depression is a mental illness and can only be treated with the right medication. Jasmine was sick. She was mentally ill."

"I was her husband. I didn't see it."

"Depressed people can live normally most of the time, seem happy, adjust to their lives ... for years even. But sometimes it just becomes too much."

They talked quietly about the subject, he told of her joy, her laughter and then her tears. He remembered the good times they had together and how he thought then that he could never love anyone.

Lyle said nothing for a while.

Melissa did not urge him to talk about it any further. She was no longer disappointed that he had never told her. Could understand how deep the pain lay, and also his guilt that he still blamed himself. Of course, he had wanted to push it away. She was all the more grateful to him now that he trusted her enough to finally open up to her. His wife. Still.

"I did everything I could to never be financially dependent again. I didn't get involved in any relationships, didn't want anything." he said powerfully now. And looked up.

Mel responded to his change of subject with a persistent tingling in her stomach. The attention now drawn back to her made her nervous, brought her back to the reality of why they were here in the first place. In any case, she remembered their first encounters. They had really failed. She would never forget the day of the accident; her scar was still visible on that knee. It had been the beginning of this complicated relationship. They had had good times too, like he had with his first wife. Would he remember her as warmly as he did Jasmine? She pushed her silly feelings of jealousy far away. It had been fifteen years. She had loved too, after all. They both had a pivotal past. Hadn't that brought them together?

"You see how love can break you. I don't want that. Not for you." Mel could not stop him as he stood up determined to get out of her reach. He tried by all means to escape her love, her future. Partly she could understand his fear, but then again, she couldn't.

"I'm not like Jasmine." she said softly, looking after him. He had his back to her.

When he didn't respond to her, she rose decisively and put her hand on his shoulder. He was tense, and once again dismissive.

But this time she knew exactly why he wanted to push her away. To *protect* her.

"Our relationship is definitely not like in your books." she continued. She had to be able to convince him. "You're not my *whole* world, Lyle. On the contrary, look at what you and I have achieved independently, this last year alone."

She stood in front of him now, still hoping he would meet her gaze. But he was withdrawing more and more from her. She felt him distancing himself further and further from her, from their relationship.

She wouldn't let him and kept talking.

"We can both move on with our lives .... successfully. These last few months have shown that. I love my work, my children, that will never change and to be honest you will always take second place to them in terms of me wanting their happiness. I've led my own life long enough; I stand on my own two feet. But enough is enough."

She sought his gaze, ignoring his cold look. Those words were clear and convincing. He had seen for himself how strong she was in her life. These four years she had never lost sight of what she wanted, what drove her. She had clear wishes, and ideas about how she could help others. And she went through with it, even without him. She was stronger than he was. All this year he had been unable to think of anything but her.

Melissa searched for the right words. Didn't want to give up.

"I can live without you. But I don't want to anymore."

"You've achieved a lot without me. You don't need me to do it."

"I don't love you because I need you, Lyle. I love you because we both want the same thing, work for the same thing, nearly break ourselves when we want something until we achieve it. You're as ambitious as I am, as unimpressed with your celebrity world as I am. You feel the same longing to *give* something to others as I do," she countered immediately. Her arguments so true, at least to her ears. "Yes, we can do our own business and lose ourselves in it. We can be really good at following rules, each to our own. But Lyle, do you still want that?"

His eyes were empty, cold. The blue seemed almost dark grey. He did not open up to her. She swam against the tide. She felt her strength running out.

"I see the pain, understand your fear. I felt so lonely, so broken when I lost my baby." she finally said, his gaze immediately locked onto hers. "I blamed myself for years. It was me who had been drinking, it was me who had stayed with that guy. The baby hadn't been able to survive because I wasn't strong enough to protect it. I swore I would never allow myself to have children. ... But then I met you and you messed everything up.....

With you, I would risk it all again. With you, I would want to experience *everything*."

Lyle closed his eyes for a few seconds.

"Melissa." he whispered almost inaudibly.

But he did not touch her, did not come closer. Did nothing. They stood inches apart, and yet it was miles.

It was only when Lyle moved that she realised she had been holding her breath. Only now did she realise she had nothing else to say. He had made up his mind.

He took the divorce papers out of the envelope and hesitated for another agonising moment. Now, in any book or film, he would tear up the documents and throw them into the air. But this was not one of his stories. It was the cruel reality they were in right now.

Lyle *signed* the papers.

"You coward." she said weakly. She could have screamed. Wanted to, and yet she showed no emotion. She wanted to appear strong, could not give in to her tears. After all, she had just claimed that she was nothing like his first wife. She would*n't* be broken by it; he wasn't her whole world.

But as good as.

"Your work as an illustrator is very much appreciated by my book publisher. Our work will still bring us together. Unless you don't want it anymore, which I would understand."

Melissa just stared at him. Torn by her questions, thoughts, intentions. Did she still want this? Could she imagine meeting him again, but not as his wife? How would she react to him then? She would never get over him then. Would that be so bad? She had no interest in falling in love with anyone. So it made no difference who lived in her heart.

Yes, she could imagine working with him.

Until he met a new woman.

Melissa stepped towards him; his gaze alarmed. He seemed unsure of what she would do. Seemed surprised or shocked when she took his pen and put her own signature next to his on the papers.

That was it.

She took a big step back. As if in a trance, barely holding herself up. But unmoved, in control. Strong.

Lyle stopped for a moment, seemed confused, wanted to say something but didn't. He looked tired, sad almost. That was all she could make out in her state. It took everything she had to hold his gaze. Even as he grabbed his jacket and took the door handle in his hand.

"Until I see you at a dull, stiff event, perhaps." he finally said. His voice weak.

She took a deep breath, tightening her posture slightly.

"I look forward to it."

Then he walked out of her flat, quietly pulling the door shut. She held her breath for a few seconds, listening intently for his footsteps. Secretly hoping he wouldn't really leave, expecting a loud knock, a change of heart. *Something.*

But then she heard the front door also fall shut. Unmistakable. He had gone. He would not be back. It was already so late, the first day in their new life had already begun. Sometime this morning he was still flying to America. That was all the time he could have spent with her. He had to go, one way or another.

Mel lost the sense of time and space. She didn't know how long she had been standing there. She closed her eyes. She should try to sleep, should come to terms with what had happened and concentrate on her work. The same as always. Nothing was different. But she couldn't get into her bed. Everything smelled of him there, the duvet, the pillows, the air. Only a few hours ago they had felt so free there, so alive, so united.

Lyle... Her heart called his name, her whole body contracted so that it hurt.

Melissa didn't move an inch, furious as a hot tear rolled down her cheek. How dare it! She wiped it away defiantly, spotting the papers still lying on the dresser beside the door. Oh great, now she had to deal with those documents too. That was the last thing she wanted to do... but she would. Tomorrow, or rather today. Immediately. Finish it, completely. No going back.

There was a knock.

She hesitated. Her stupid heart hoping. Her mind explaining.

The papers, he wasn't leaving them behind after all. Fortunately. Wasn't it? There was no other reason why he should be at her door again. *Don't do this to yourself*. Forget it.

She found the strength to open the door for him, to hand him the envelope and watch him leave again. Couldn't find the strength to win him over. Her hopes lay in ruins at her feet.

He stood before her. Misery written all over his face.

"I can't go like this," he said weakly.

Wordlessly she stood before him, refusing to open her whole heart to him once again. Everything in her *yearned* for him, for his love. But her mind was screaming at her, admonishing her so loudly that she could not hear her heart and was completely powerless. How should she react? Should she once again give everything to convince him that they were meant for each other? *He had to want it himself.* She didn't want to have to *persuade* him, *force* him into a relationship with her. That was the very last thing she could cope with. It would only lead to her unhappiness. Now was the best time to draw a line. As soon as he left, she could start healing.

"Ask me again." he urged her softly, stepping closer. He seemed not at all himself. Deepest pain in his eyes. Despair in his voice. All aversion, all distance blown away and before her was a broken man. "Ask me how I feel."

Melissa swallowed in surprise. Torn by her own turmoil.

"Do you love me?" Her voice broke as she struggled with herself. Her stomach clenched painfully. Her throat was so dry. She didn't dare breathe, hope, ...believe.

"Yes."

And he fell into her arms. Completely weak and suffering. He sought hold in *her* embrace, in *her* love as he had never needed it before.

Both sank to their knees. Neither could find the words to describe exactly what they felt. Silent tears ran down their cheeks. Neither stopped them from falling, neither had the strength to hide their feelings. She knew that at that moment he was not only crying for her, but also for his past. He had to finally release these pent-up feelings, these feelings of endless guilt, and forgive himself. He had never given himself that chance. He was overwhelmed with what he felt he should do.

"I love you ... so much it scares me." he whispered into the night. He clung to her, so tightly that she didn't know if he was holding her or Jasmine. "What if I disappoint you? What if I can't give you what you want? What if you become sad? Can't laugh anymore. I would never forgive myself for that. I don't know if I should risk it."

Melissa's heart was pounding so loudly. She was trembling all over, a thousand emotions falling on her at once. She gently pushed him away from her to be able to look into his eyes. His eyes, his tears. It was unbearable to see him like that. She put her hands around his face and stroked the tears from his cheeks with her thumb. Her gaze remained strong, though her own eyes had given in to her emotions for a moment.

"You're already doing it. You're here."

Lyle awkwardly wiped the remaining tears from his eyes with his sleeve. He inhaled deeply and exhaled again. The anguish was still in his eyes, but he saw her. Clear and distinct and so stunningly strong. A few tiny traces of her tears were still visible in her lashes. But the brown of her eyes still shone assuring and he could lose himself deeply in her. She was holding him in that moment. She showed him what it meant to love and to live. Why hadn't he seen it before, that she was the reason he always felt empty without her? How many times had he lied to himself and repressed that attraction when it was all he needed to be happy and forgive himself?

"You're not like her." he finally said. His voice slowly fuller and more convinced. She felt him regain his own self and he built himself up. To the man she had instantly fallen in love with years ago. And could do it again in an instant.

"And no, I don't love her anymore. Not the way you think I do."

As soon as she met his gaze and heard his warm voice, those

stupid tears sprang to her eyes again. She defied them with all her might and was helpless. For years she had not given tears a chance. For years she had been strong and then he comes along and breaks her. But she hadn't been the only one... he had cried over her too.

Lyle straightened up and pulled her up with him. He went to the door to close it. Something that had completely slipped her mind. When he turned to face her again, his shoulders were taut. His head was up and he was Lyle McClory again.

With an intriguing smile on his lips.

"This whole evening is crazy. Our marriage ... ." He ran a tired hand through his hair and over his face. He had confessed his love to her, a huge milestone, and what a feeling it gave her. Relief, hope, joy, pride. Now all that was missing was the feeling of happiness that he could also choose to want to live with it. To want to live with *her*. He still hadn't spoken any clarities, or spoken out *in favour* of a relationship with her. She still found herself in absolute no man's land and she was tired of it. She was so tired, so infinitely tired, her temper flared up again inside. Give us a chance or not. No matter what now, but she couldn't stand another back and forth like this. What now?

What she had hoped for from his reappearance still hadn't come. She grew angrier by the second. What was he coming in here like this, forcing her to her knees, crying a little, rebuilding himself and then what? Then bitterly disappoint her again?

"The papers are there. What more do you want?" she replied tersely. Her tone was appropriately annoyed. "You love me, I love you. Now what?"

"I wanted to add something." he replied seriously, ignoring the envelope. He moved closer and tried to stroke her cheek. She turned her face away determinedly. Her eyes flashed menacingly at him. He did not let it get him down.

"We don't need to do anything anymore. Our marriage is over."

"Yes, this marriage is over." he confirmed and she frowned.

It hurt to hear it. She was completely confused as to what he wanted or didn't want now. Everything inside her screamed and tugged. She had had enough!

"It's over."

He sounded so relieved. He stood there, completely unmoved by her, by her confessions and he smiled? Did he not see her despair, her grief, her fucking tears? Was he making fun of her? This man was driving her absolutely crazy!

Lyle exhaled deeply, grabbed her arms and ignored the way she tried to push him away. Now it was his turn to talk. He had suddenly found such strength within himself that he couldn't order his thoughts at all. He wanted to cheer and celebrate and take her. But it was more important to be patient for a moment, he had to win her over. Fully convinced of his intentions.

"I can't deny how much I want you. You make me mad; you drive me crazy and .... you make me laugh."

Melissa's eyes snapped open. He spoke from her soul.

Her movements paused; her defences weakened. She listened to every word.

"I want you to always tell me what you think and think of me. I *never* want you to change for me."

He moved closer to her, now completely without resistance on her part. So close that she felt his hot breath on her face. Everything inside her contracted. Her silly heart was awake again and anxious.

"I want to be close to you, wherever we are. I want your scent on my skin so that you are always with me when we are kept apart. I want to be able to touch you and ignite that fire in you that you ignite in me."

His kiss was passionate and sensual. She felt it all the way into her soul. She thought for a brief moment that he had never kissed her like that before. Then she could think no more. Her whole body responded. Without hesitation, she put her arms around his neck and opened herself to his love. Her knees were so soft she was afraid she wouldn't be able to stand.

Lyle interrupted this moment reluctantly. His breath was faltering, his eyes so dark, full of the deepest emotion. He leaned his forehead briefly on hers to steady himself.

"I want..." he swallowed. "I wish for you to marry me because you love me and I love you, so infinitely. No contract. Just the two of us. ... Melissa, what do you think, will you be my wife?"

Melissa didn't move for a moment, couldn't breathe. Her heart was still racing from the kiss. Her mind needed a moment to come back down to earth and digest *all* his words. His love, his honesty, his willingness to spend his life with her. Lyle wanted her completely now, after all. If he hadn't held her in his arms, she would have fallen to her knees again. But he gave *her* support this time. He was so powerful in his nature, in his words. He was an incredibly attractive, irritating, passionate man whom she never wanted to let go.

A relieved laugh escaped her as his words really struck her.

Lyle ran his thumb over her moist lips, over her smile. Felt her open to him completely, and enjoyed, the deep tug in his own heart as he did too.

"Are you saying yes?"

Mel kissed him instead, all her love flowing into their kiss. She felt overwhelming happiness. She felt joyful and free. Free from worry, free from pain and misery, free from having to *suppress* anything. It was a unique feeling, just as good as his hands on her body.

"Oh yes ... I marry you ... only you.... Oh yes ... today ... tomorrow..." came her words, so convincing, so warm, between kisses and breaths.

Lyle pressed her body against him, never wanting to let her go.

"Third time lucky!" he said, seeing her confused look. "The first time you passed out, the second time I left you reeling on our wedding bed and this time ... this time it's like in my books."

She smiled at his comparison. Yes, all those moments had led them here. What a roller coaster. She wouldn't change a thing about it. *Nothing.*

Mel rested her head against his shoulder, just for a few seconds. She couldn't quite believe her luck. She had to calm down. She would fall over if she didn't. Everything inside her jumped with joy and pure lust surged through at his seductive touch on her back. She inhaled deeply. Ah his aftershave was so dear to her; she had missed it so.

Something still worried her though and she plucked up the courage to address it.

"And your inheritance?" she reminded herself the moment she could think of anything. Her question was hesitant and cautious. Her eyes large and concerned. "We can still tear up the papers and just have a fake wedding?"

She would do anything for him, including continue this show marriage. With him by her side, she could endure anything. Even Angela and Verona, press articles and interviews, nothing scared her anymore.

"No, I don't want to keep playing games." he said firmly, his look sincere, without regret. Then he told her about the last year, about his deals and negotiations. Mel was speechless.

"I asked you for this year so I had enough time to infuse the money into several projects. A large part of it goes indirectly to your company. I have negotiated several plans and contracts that will help out children in your name. I just needed time to do it."

Melissa didn't know if it was possible, but at that moment she loved him even *more*. Not only for the projects he had started in the interest of hundreds of thousands of children, but also that he really didn't want this fake act anymore. He really wanted to marry her, Melissa, and give them a real chance.

"And your new contracts in America?"

"I'm putting them on hold for a while. I'll stay here for now and work from here. I have some other pressing needs. ... Even if I'm only *second* in line."

They both laughed, something they had done so rarely. It felt incredibly good.

"Lyle... I just want to be your wife now." she said from the bottom of her heart. "Your acquaintances will be running their mouths. Angela especially, she'll hate me even more. And Verona ... I only hope she found the same happiness with Richard."

"There'll be some stiff events where we should be there. You can shove it under their noses then."

"Maybe I can give you more affection than is allowed." She kissed him seductively on the mouth. Everything in him craved her. He loved it when she knew no shyness.

"And you ... you're looking forward to it?" he said teasingly and Mel laughed lightly. "I rip your heart out and you say I look forward to it? Go do one or ... fuck you, something like that would have been more appropriate. I certainly deserved it."

She smiled, tears in her eyes.

"Yeah, do me..." she replied, amused. She teased him with her mouth, biting his lips lightly, and again. "Over and over again."

Her kiss was full of lust and relief. She pulled his head towards her and deepened her kiss to drive him mad. Her hands grabbed his top and pulled it up, over his head.

Lyle was overwhelmed by his feelings, pressing her against him and fully conforming to her lust. His hands slid under her blouse, feeling her hot smooth skin. She moaned softly as he kissed her neck. He slipped the thin fabric off her body without hindrance.

"Melissa, how did you ever manage to make me lose myself in you?" he whispered. Between his words, his lips caressed the tender skin in the hollow of her neck. He loved hearing her make those sweet little sounds. He was crazy about her. "Ever since the day you stood in my hospital room, you've enchanted me. You in your jeans and blouses. Like you did again today. After all I had sworn myself ... I tried everything not to let you into my heart."

"I understand why." she said quietly, running her hand down his cheek. "Understand you."

"You are one of a kind." His kiss was now gentle and loving, his gaze serious. "You're right, we should both get over our loss. Create new life."

Mel felt a thrilling tingle in her belly. She felt like she was floating.

"But not by ourselves." she demanded forcefully.

"Like I could leave you alone." His body was pressed tightly against her, needing her close as much as she needed him at that moment.

"You used to disappear for weeks at a time."

"The worst times of my life. Those weeks all alone in a stupid hotel room, with my mind on you. I couldn't bear your sheer presence, wanting so badly to pull you close to me and do exactly what I have in mind now...."

Melissa looked seductively into his eyes, they shone with happiness and joy.

"Did you fall in love with me years ago?"

"Head over heels."

They both laughed at his answer. Finally, the fear was conquered and the truth was out.

~ DAS ENDE ~

ABOUT THE AUTHOR

Susann Svoboda

Growing up in East Germany, I wrote my first stories as a teenager. In my lessons, secretly but perhaps not unnoticed, I scribbled my never-ending declaration of love for Gary Barlow, which soon developed into one love story after another on the backs of our English tests and worksheets. Having always been fascinated by England and its language, I preferred to use English names for my characters from the start.

Now almost twenty years later, I have found the time and courage to revisit these stories and also publish them.

Therefore, the original ideas and dialogue came from a dreamy young girl; but the present stories come from me as a mother of three young girls who will soon be fantasizing about their own idols. Together with my husband, we live in England and hope with these stories to give you something to dream along too.

BOOKS IN THIS SERIES

ant matters. Why had Lyle chosen her to spend the rest of his life with? What was she doing in this high society? Did she actually belong here?

BOOKS BY THIS AUTHOR

When The Past Destroys Hope

Jeff Knights already had his hands full - his farm was about to harvest and needed every single ounce of its proceeds to survive, and then Valerie Heffron showed up. The dolled-up millionaire's daughter who could buy anything she desired with her money. She was the girl he had wanted to marry.
And suddenly she was standing in front of him, completely without glamour and designer clothes. But he could see through her games. She was still the same, spoilt girl from back then. However, he had to admit that she was no longer a girl. She was an irritating woman who made no sign of wanting to leave his farm, no matter how often they got in each other's way.

www.ingramcontent.com/pod-product-compliance
Lightning Source LLC
Chambersburg PA
CBHW071610150726
48000CB00004B/1654